M.J. Raco, a mother of three and grandmother to one, lives in South-Western Sydney, Australia. She has dedicated over thirty years of her life to helping save and restore the sight of thousands of patients in Australia and Fiji.

Realm Travellers

A Parallel Dimension

M.J. Raco

AIA PUBLISHING

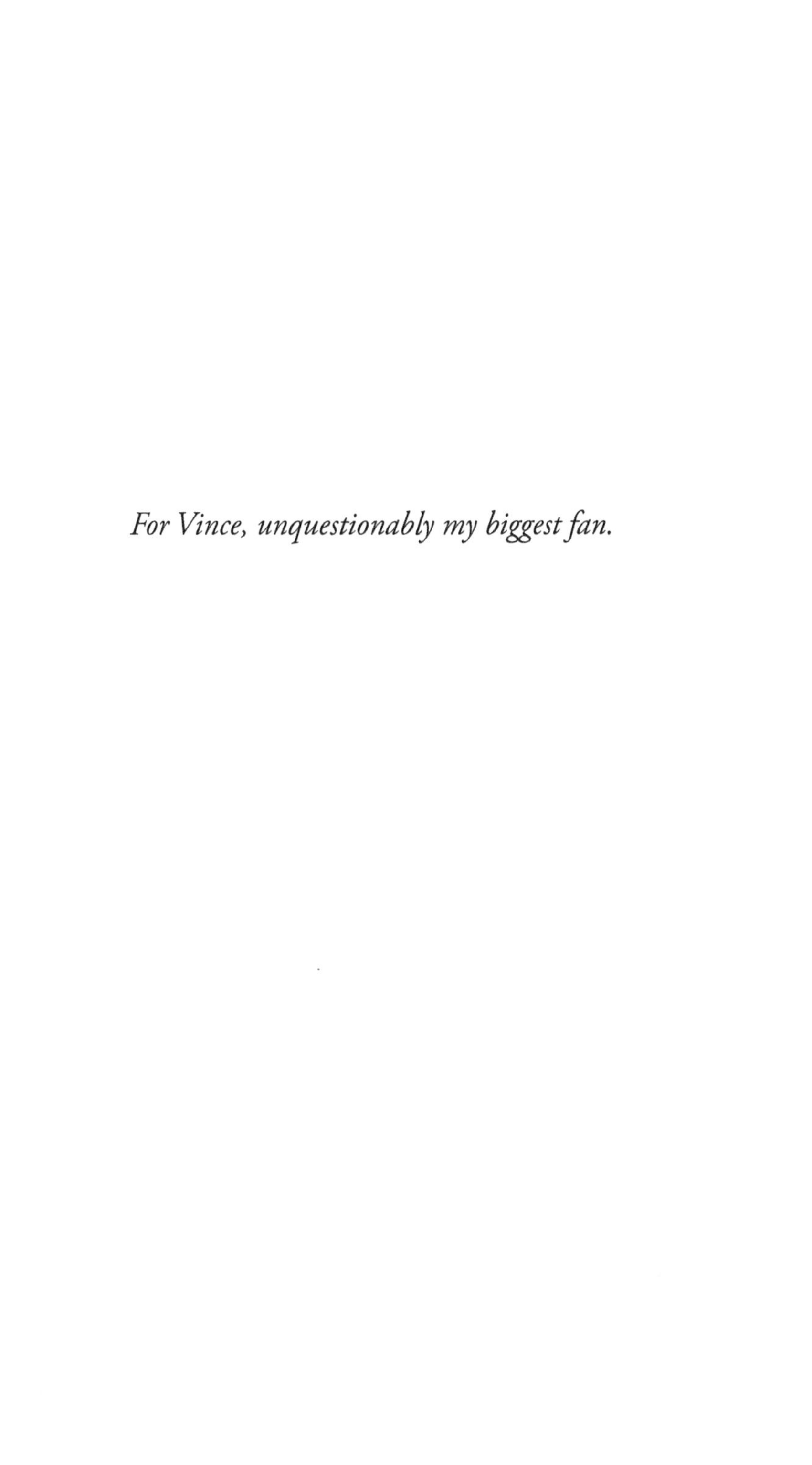

For Vince, unquestionably my biggest fan.

Acknowledgements

I need to start by thanking my biggest supporter, husband and best friend, Vince. From the beginning of this amazing journey, you've been there by my side, eager to sing my praises but also ready to pick me up each time I've faltered. You're my rock, and I love you, your heart, and the amazing person you are.

To my gorgeous children, Stephanie, Michael and Alec, you are by far the best gifts God has given me, for which I give thanks every day. For all that you are and all that you do, I thank you with all of my heart: Stephanie with your encouragement and guidance; Michael with your patience and creative vision, and Alec with your honesty and direction. Your pride in me fuels the burning flame within to follow my dreams. But most importantly thank you for the love you give unconditionally.

A huge thankyou goes to the awesome team at AIA Publishing who helped bring my books to life: Tahlia for your never-ending support and guidance which has been truly treasured, and to the ever-patient Rose for your receptivity and brilliant creativity.

GLOSSARY

ASIO: Australian Security Intelligence Organisation

Aussie: Australian (pronounced 'Ozzie')

Fair dinkum: true, genuine

Gobsmacked: surprised, astounded

Larrikin: a boisterous, often badly behaved young man

OTT: over the top

SES: State Emergency Services

Shit scared: so scared I could poo in my pants

Stoked: very pleased

I

WHITE NOISE

JACK

Jack lands on the ground with a thud. Thankfully, falling on Peanut cushions the impact somewhat, but the stabbing pain that shoots through his side feels almost unbearable. The intensity of it is so overwhelming, he can't breathe, and he bites down on his tongue to stop himself from crying out. It takes him a moment to regain his composure, but once there, he carefully releases a jagged breath.

Peanut jumps to his feet, immediately on the defensive. He glances around, taking in the situation.

The first thing Jack becomes aware of, other than his pain, is the fresh smell of eucalyptus. And then he hears the familiar sound of the currawongs. He looks up at the trees and surveys the forest. They've made it; they're home.

Ruby rushes out of the bushes at Peanut and almost bowls him over. 'Thank God you got away. But where are the others?'

Peanut wraps his arms around her. 'They're right behind us. Hey, are you okay?' He lets her go briefly to look her over.

'I'm good, but what about Max, and Ryker?' she asks with an anxious furrow in her brow.

Kenny, Edra and the twins emerge from their hiding place, clearly a little ruffled from the ordeal but keen to hear what's going on.

'Ryker's at the gateway, ready to pass,' Peanut says, 'and Max isn't far behind. They'll be here any second. You'll see.'

'Then, guys, be ready,' Kenny warns, 'the guards could fall through with them.' He grabs a broken branch and prepares himself for what might follow. The others do the same.

Jack presses his hand to his wound and with Peanut's help, moves to safety. From a distance, he watches and waits for Ryker and Max.

But nothing happens. The gossamer curtain, suspended untethered, waves gently at them, emitting no one.

Jack staggers forward, clutching at his side. 'Max?'

he calls out.

But too much time has passed. Something has gone terribly wrong.

'Max!'

The others are by his side in moments, staring in disbelief at the diaphanous veil. Not one of them is able to utter a single word.

Ruby falls to her knees, grief-stricken, and starts to sob. Peanut kneels beside her and wraps her in his arms.

Jack wavers, on the brink of collapsing. Kenny helps him to a nearby log.

Suddenly a scream alerts them of danger. Jack turns to see Ulan pointing nervously at the portal.

'It's a guard! I just saw him stick his head through.'

'Take cover and be ready to attack!' Banji cries out, and they all scatter to find a safe hiding place.

But before Jack has a chance to get away, two guards stumble through the portal. They scramble to their feet and stand ready, their keen eyes surveying the area. Jack makes a run for it, but the pain from his wound tells him he won't be able to get away quick enough. He searches for something to protect himself with, sees a rock, grabs it, and hurls it at the troll of a guard who's hot on his tail. The rock hits him in the face, stopping him momentarily in his tracks. But the second guard isn't far behind. Heart thumping, Jack looks around for something else to use.

But then, Peanut charges out of the underbrush with a broken branch at the ready to take on Jack's attacker. He wacks the second guard from behind with his weapon, sending him face first into the ground. He then jumps onto him and pounds the back of his head—relentlessly.

A sudden upsurge of attackers appears from the bushes. Armed with crude weapons, all the kids join the assault on the guards.

Jack watches on helplessly. The kids outnumber the guards, but he's not stupid enough to think they've got the upper hand. These guys are strong, so they're not out of danger yet. But, strangely, the guards struggle to fight back and, surprisingly, within seconds, the kids wear them down. What happens next is beyond anything Jack could have anticipated. The guards throw off their assailants and make a run for it. But they don't re-enter the portal, instead they tear off to find shelter in the unknown of the national park.

'Oh my God,' Ruby says. 'We've got to go after them.'

'And do what?' Kenny asks, panting from his efforts. 'We can't overpower them. And what are we supposed to do when or, more to the point, *if* we catch up to them? Let's just focus on getting us out of here first. We can worry about them later.'

Jack's head starts to spin, and suddenly he's feeling light-headed. He staggers off to find somewhere to sit.

'Hey, are you okay?' Peanut follows, catches him before he falls and eases him onto a fallen log.

Jack drops his head between his knees and tries to control his breathing. 'Where's Max?' he asks in a shaky voice, reminding them that they haven't all passed through. The likelihood of them still being alive now is almost zero.

Once again they're stunned into a grave silence.

'No! It can't end like this.' Jack fights to stand up, and then staggers towards the portal. 'I'm not giving up. We've gotta do something—anything. Max!'

Peanut, still by his side, looks down at Jack's blood-drenched shirt. 'Dude, you need to sit for a bit while we work out what to do here.' He helps him back to the log.

With his elbows on his knees and head cradled in his hands, Jack closes his eyes and tries to lose himself in a fog of white noise. Who's he kidding? Max is gone. His insides turn to ice.

Peanut squats down next to Jack and places his hands firmly on his shoulders, urging him to look at him, 'Mate, listen to me; she's with Ryker. They're okay, all right?'

His words sound foggy and distant to Jack, and he struggles to gain any depth of meaning.

But they clearly have an effect on Banji. 'Hey, you're right,' he says, suddenly excited. 'Guys, think about it. We're talking about Ryker, here. Edra, Ulan, you guys know him as well as I do. He wouldn't have risked taking on so many guards. He would've seen that the odds were stacked against them, grabbed Max, and made a run for it. They've probably already outrun the guards and are at this very moment in hiding.' Banji's words slowly make their way to Jack's consciousness.

What? She could still be alive?

Hope glimmers bright for a moment, but then he remembers how weak she was, and a cloud of doubt looms over him. 'There's no way she could've kept up with him. After helping me, she was totally wasted. I've seen the effect these healings have on her. All her strength gets drained.'

'Yeah, but don't forget, Ryker's strong enough for both of them,' Ulan reassures him. 'Besides, he'd never let anything happen to her. She means too much to him.'

'And what's that supposed to mean!' Jack hears himself lash out.

Ulan recoils, startled by his sudden outburst.

And she's not the only one. Jack can't believe his

own overreaction.

'Hey, I know you're hurting right now,' she says sympathetically, 'but believe me, she's in good hands. Ryker would do anything for her. It took a near-death experience for him to realise the monster he'd become. He owes her his life.'

A myriad of conflicting emotions instantly consume Jack's thoughts. Hearing that the chances are good that Max is safe is the best news in the world, but for some reason, knowing that she's alone with Ryker has him seething with jealousy. He shakes his head. *What the hell is with this sudden cave-man mentality!*

'I'm with you guys,' Edra tells them. 'Ryker isn't an idiot. He wouldn't have risked getting caught.'

'So what you're all saying is that there's hope,' Peanut confirms, just to drive home the point for Jack. 'In that case we need to keep positive about what's going on back there. We've got to believe they're still alive.'

Ruby wipes away the tears from her eyes. 'So what are we doing just standing around? They need our help!'

Jack snaps out of it. His selfish deliberations only delay their rescue. 'What do you reckon we should do?'

'There's got to be a search-party nearby looking

for us, don't ya think?' Peanut says, 'Maybe Kenny and I should go look for 'em.'

'Sounds like a plan,' Kenny says decisively. 'There's a good chance the searchers have set up a base at the campsite, so we should start there.'

The others agree. Peanut and Kenny are to make their way there, while the rest remain to guard the portal.

Ulan frowns. 'But what happens if the guards come back? We won't be able to fight them off.'

Peanut chuckles. 'If they come back, I reckon that after that last beating we gave 'em, they'll be more interested in getting out of here than chasing after you lot. I wouldn't worry if I were you.'

'Come on,' Kenny says, keen to get going. 'Let's go. Just stick together guys, and you'll be okay.' He and Peanut head off.

'And Jack,' Peanut calls back, 'don't do anything stupid. We don't want you undoing all of Max's hard work, okay? Remember that you've just lost your superpowers, and you're back to being a kid who's only now had an arrow pulled out of his chest.'

Jack smiles. 'Okay, okay. I'll just sit here and wait. Happy? Now get the hell out of here.'

He watches as Kenny and Peanut climb the slope of the ravine, retracing the steps they took so many days ago. He wishes he was going with them, but he's useless to them like this. Peanut is right; he needs to rest. Max would want that too.

I'll do it for Max.

'You're thinking about her, aren't you?' Ulan quietly asks him.

Caught by surprise at the question, Jack says, 'I thought we'd lost our superpowers.'

She smiles. 'Don't look so worried; I can't read your thoughts. It's just that I'm naturally intuitive,' she tells him. 'Besides, I've seen that look on your face before. She's a special person, your Max.'

And at that moment he realises just how special she is … especially to him.

2

ℱ‌AITH

Ryker

Ryker stands next to the transparent, floating portal. He's just fought off one of the guards, and everyone has safely escaped the Ancient Realm—everyone that is, except for Max. She's too far out of his reach for him to save her. And there's no way she'll make it to him on her own. She can't; she's too weak. It's obvious that she's struggling to even hold herself upright.

But her eyes, although heavy with exhaustion, are begging him to go, to take that final plunge and save himself.

He's so close to finally being free. Four torturous years in this hell-hole, and all he needs to do is to fall through the wispy veil, and he'll be there. He'll be safe.

The guards are standing again, having recovered from their sudden, mysterious fall, and he has only seconds before they're upon him. He looks at his options, searching Max's pleading eyes, then looking back at the veil. He needs to make a decision, and fast—save himself or save Max?

But it's a no-brainer. It's Max. *It'll always be Max.*

He takes off, not stopping to look back, and before she has time to protest, he scoops Max into his arms and runs for their lives. He ploughs through the forest, oblivious to the branches ripping at his arms and face. Tree roots threaten to mar his progress, but none of that distracts him from his focus. His mind is set on one objective—to escape capture. His gaze darts around, scoping the area for any further threat, and since he knows the area well now, he takes familiar paths.

Max clings to him, her face buried in his chest. But she's safe. He won't let her fall.

The wind in his ears muffles all other sounds apart from his laboured breathing. But then, suddenly, he picks up on distant cries from the guards in pursuit. His pace surges. There's no way he's going to let the guards get anywhere near them.

He takes several sharp turns, running deeper into

the forest, trying to shake off their pursuers. They move into denser vegetation, slowing a little, and Ryker soon secures them a hiding place in a hollow, secreted behind some large-leafed plants. The light is heavily filtered and dim, providing them with temporary refuge.

Ryker tries to control his loud breathing. He closes his eyes, listening for signs of a chase … but he hears none. Allowing himself to relax a little, he looks down at Max, nestled against his chest. Her eyes, wide with fear, reflects his own state of alert. He consciously masks his alarm, and her tension softens as a result. She looks so small and fragile in his arms. He can't even begin to imagine seeing himself through her eyes.

What must she think of me? I've been nothing but a monster to her!

His self-loathing makes him turn away from her trusting eyes. He doesn't deserve her faith in him.

'I'm sorry,' she whispers.

What? He's momentarily stunned.

'I know you're annoyed. It's my fault you're stuck here.'

He can't believe it; she's mistaken his withdrawal as a look of resentment. 'No, you've got it wrong. Believe me, it's not you I'm angry with. I could never be mad at you, Maxine.'

She frowns. 'Why did you call me that? Nobody calls me Maxine.'

She's caught him out. He squirms from embarrassment, forces a smile and motions to her that they should keep quiet. She doesn't pursue it any further, and for that he's more than a little relieved. The effort required to keep her eyes open is obvious. She closes them, relaxes against him and falls asleep within seconds.

Ryker looks down at her, resting peacefully, and lets go some of the tension created in the past few hours. Knowing they'll be here for a while, he tries to get comfortable. If they make it through the night, he's confident that the guards will back off. They know too well what's out here. In their eyes, to be exiled into the forest will be punishment enough.

He closes his eyes and listens to the sounds of the night, and very quickly dozes off.

3

ℳAXINE

RYKER

A chilling scream in the middle of the night has Ryker suddenly wide awake. It's Max. She's squirming in his arms, and in the filtered moonlight, he sees a look of terror in her eyes.

'Hey, shh; it's okay. Max, it's all right.' He tries to pacify her, but she continues to struggle against him. Her arms thrash aimlessly, and her breathing is erratic. He realises she's having a nightmare and continues to calm her by gently shushing and holding her. Slowly her body relaxes, the nightmare subsides, and she falls back into a restful sleep.

He looks at her innocent face, a reminder of her vulnerability, and reflects on the effect this whole

14

ordeal must have had on her—and his barbarian actions haven't done her any favours either.

She's what, fifteen? Sixteen? The horrors she's just lived through would leave anyone scarred. Hell, I'm twenty-one, and I know I'll never be the same.

'I'll always look after you, Maxine,' he whispers to her. 'I owe you that much.' He eases her closer to him, securing her in his arms. The warmth he feels from that simple gesture brings him inexplicable comfort, and he allows himself, for the first time in a long time, to quietly indulge in it.

But he doesn't go to sleep again. He curses himself for falling asleep in the first place. *'Vigilant at all times.' What's wrong with you!*

He lays awake listening to the sounds of the night. Small unseen animals scurry in the woods, hunting for a meal. He takes a moment to reflect on his past life. This place is such a contrast to what he knew and grew up with. Back home, or at least in the Kruger National Park where he was before disappearing into the Realm, he'd be listening to the faraway sounds of restless lions or flighty hyenas. He smiles confidently, knowing there's no such threat out here. Ryker sighs deeply. At this moment in time, the world seems to be at peace and, despite their situation, the stillness of the forest makes him feel safe.

The chirp of a bird or two alerts Ryker to the

break of day. The sounds of dawn seem like a deep cleansing of his soul—a chance for renewal.

He lays a hand gently on Max's shoulder and gives a little shake. 'Hey, it's time for us to get going. Wake up, sleepyhead.'

She wakes in a fright and jerks out of Ryker's hold. Her pupils are dilated, her breathing suddenly frantic, and her hands fly up, ready to fight.

'Whoa, hold on. You're okay. You're with me. We're safe.'

Recall slowly dawns on her, and she relaxes. 'Wow, we made it!'

'Yeah, we made it.'

'So now what?' She gives him a questioning look.

'Now, we get going. I know a place, and it's safe. You know how we've been in the forest for a week now? Well, we've built a tree house, and we can stay there until we're rescued. It's not that far.'

He starts to ease himself up, but Max grabs at his shirt, suddenly frightened. 'But what about the forest people?'

'What about them?'

'What if we come across them? Aren't they savage?' Her hold on him tightens.

Ryker can't help but smile at her innocence. 'Like I said, we've been in the forest for a week now, and we've been able to manage without too much trouble.

Look, don't get me wrong; what you've been told by the guards about them is basically true, some of them are savage, but there are some you can trust, too.'

Her tense posture relaxes a little.

'A lot of them know what we're planning, so they're looking out for us. Although,' he says as an afterthought, 'I guess the situation's a bit different now. With what happened in the arena, we might have a price on our heads, and some might be tempted to hunt us down. You guys really left the place in a mess, and I'm guessing that more than a few people got hurt. So maybe we shouldn't be so trusting.'

'Oh.' Max takes in his words in silence for a moment before asking, 'What did you mean when you said that they know what you're planning? What, exactly, are you doing?'

Ryker looks at her incredulously and almost laughs. 'Me? Hey, it wasn't my idea to organise a mass exodus. I vaguely remember it being yours.'

'Me!' she echoes, then realises his meaning. 'What? They already know?'

'Yeah.' He chuckles. 'And believe it or not, some of them are seriously thinking of coming back with us. Amazing, hey?'

'Wow!'

'We've formed a kind of alliance with them.'

'Double wow!'

Ryker scratches his head. 'How is it that you're so surprised?'

'Well,' she laughs nervously, 'can you blame me?' His blank look prompts her to explain. 'It's not so much about finding that they want to come back with us—that, I get—it's more that you've actually done something about it. No offense, Ryker, but you weren't the most agreeable person when we first met. I couldn't see you being behind the idea. I knew Edra, Ulan and Banji were on board with it, but you? Well, no way did I see that coming.'

Ryker inwardly groans. He can't blame her for thinking that. But that was then. 'I'm not that person anymore, Max. That's all in the past … you've changed me.'

Her eyes widen hearing this. She clears her throat, visibly uncomfortable with his familiarity. 'Well then, that's kind of awesome,' she says awkwardly. 'So, um, you've convinced them, then?'

He recognises her attempt to divert the conversation, and gives himself a mental warning to hold back from being so personal. 'Yeah, something like that,' he mumbles, feeling stupid.

Unexpectedly, Max's face lights up with happiness. 'Ryker, you're amazing. Thank you. This means so much.' Her smile instantly erases yet another embarrassing moment. 'These battles are just so wrong, aren't they? It's totally barbaric the way The Ancients treat these poor people. It needs to stop.'

True, but it's not the forest people he's thinking of that makes Ryker suddenly giddy; it's seeing a glow of happiness light up her beautiful face, and knowing he was the one who put it there. He lowers his face to secretly savour the moment.

But there's no time for that now. They need to make tracks. He clears his throat. 'Are you ready?'

'Absolutely.' Her eyes gleam with enthusiasm. 'Let's go check out this treehouse of yours.'

/ 4

ᕼUGGIES

MAX

Max follows quietly as Ryker leads them through the woods. Ideas and plans for getting the forest people out safely fill her head. She's on a high—who would've thought that Ryker would turn out to be so friendly and helpful. She looks at him in amazement and wonders how she was ever frightened of him. He's right; he's a completely different person to the monster he was before. *Not such a beast after all …*

She shakes the thoughts from her head and tries to focus on keeping up with him as he forges a path to the treehouse. He's on a mission. That much is clear. His gaze darts everywhere, continuously on the lookout. She admires his thorough and methodical surveillance. It's still a little dark, but that doesn't appear to bother him. She, on the other hand, struggles to keep herself from tripping over and landing flat on her face. She senses he's had some kind of military training—or maybe four years in this place gives you no option but to be combat-ready.

Not once, as they make their way through the forest, does he hesitate to reconsider their path. 'Ryker,' she asks, surprised at his familiarity with the terrain, 'how is it that you know where we're going? Each tree looks the same to me.'

'We've gotten to know the forest pretty well, now, especially the area around the gateway. We needed to be prepared for anything. The chances of us failing were pretty high, so I invested several man-hours scouring the area and familiarising myself with recognisable landmarks.'

Max stops. *Oh yeah, military training, all right!*

Ryker turns and laughs at her expression. 'Um, maybe I need to explain that I spent six years in the sea cadets back home, and I specialised in survival training for two of those years.'

She needs a moment to digest this. 'You mean to tell me that your parents sent you to a military school as soon as you graduated from being in Huggies?'

He looks at her in confusion. 'I'm not sure what

you mean by Huggies. Is that some sort of academy back in Australia?'

Max laughs at the serious expression on his face … like he's trying to solve an important puzzle. 'Relax, it's just a joke. Huggies are what you'd call nappies or diapers. I only meant that I'm surprised that you've already done so much in your life. Are you always this intense?'

He laughs at himself. 'Yeah, I guess I am. Edra is always at me about that. Her favourite line is "Take a chill-pill, Ryker!"' He mimics her. 'I guess this place messes with your head after a while. It's pretty hard not to take everything so seriously.'

'No drama, I get it.'

He smiles at her. 'You Aussies have a weird way of saying things sometimes. No drama,' he repeats. 'I guess it's like saying no problem, right?'

She nods and smiles at the solemn expression on his face.

He frowns, deep in thought for a moment. 'Going back to that Huggies question, my parents are pretty cool; they never made me do anything. I had the chance to join the cadets when I was in grade six, so I took it. You see, I come from a military background. My father is a marine and so was his father before him. So I was naturally inclined to join the forces, too. Dad suggested I do a few years as a cadet so I'd have a chance to see what I'd be up for, and I reckon he secretly hoped I'd get it out of my system and then follow a safer career path. That's where I was before stumbling across this place. I was in my first year at uni, studying geography. One day I'm going to be a teacher, just like my mother.'

'A teacher! Get out of town! I did not see that one coming.'

Ryker laughs at her reaction.

Max thinks about her own father and can't imagine having a relationship like his. 'Well, I guess you're lucky to have such a supportive father,' she says, suddenly sullen.

She changes the direction of their conversation before he picks up on her bitterness and starts asking prying questions. 'What other words do you have trouble understanding? By the way, I love your accent.'

'Accent? I don't have an accent. But you do.' He grins. 'And it's kind of cute. I like listening to you talk. As for misunderstanding you, I don't have that much trouble with what you say, but I will confess that Peanut had my head spinning most of the time.'

Max laughs because she can certainly see where he's coming from.

'For example,' he says, 'what on earth does "fair dinkum" mean? I've heard Peanut use it a few times, and can't quite get my head around its meaning.'

'That's an expression we use for something that's genuine or true.'

Ryker considers her explanation for a moment. 'So, Max, you fair dinkum think I have an accent?'

Max giggles at his attempt. 'Not bad,' she lies. 'Stick around and I'll have you talking Aussie-speak in no time.'

He reaches out for her hand to help guide them through the forest. Strangely, it feels natural, so she allows it, and they walk on.

The journey soon becomes a little easier as rays of light start to filter through the trees and show the way. Before long they're standing at the foot of a well-concealed treehouse. Max looks up at the underside of it in complete and utter awe.

Wow! He built this?

She doesn't have time to process how on earth they're going to get up there. He starts climbing the massive tree using nothing but a vine strapped around his waist, virtually bunny-hopping all the way up. Once up in the treehouse, he throws down a rope made of plaited vines, and quickly climbs down, landing at her feet.

She jumps back alarmed. *Is this guy for real!*

'It was definitely easier when Edra just jumped up for the rope.' He laughs, not even close to being out of breath. 'Climb on board; I'll take you up.' He squats on his haunches so she can jump on his back.

Max feels her face turn bright red with embarrassment. 'I don't expect you to carry me everywhere we go. Just show me how to do it, and I'll have a go myself.'

'It's not that easy,' he says. 'It takes heaps of arm and core strength to haul your own body weight.'

Geez, what kind of caveman mentality is that!

Her offence must have been clearly written on her face because he resorts to trying a different approach. 'Look, I'll show you some other time. How about for now I get you to safety? Hop on,' he offers again.

Reluctantly, Max climbs onto his back, and he effortlessly hauls both their weights up the tree in seconds. She realises the strength needed to achieve what he'd just done and feels stupid for ever thinking she could do it. She'd never be able to manage it, not even on her best day.

'There's no shame in not being able to do things, you know,' he tells her, as if reading her mind. 'So don't be so hard on yourself. I'm here to help you, so just let me.'

That'll be a challenge for her—letting someone do something for her instead of doing it for herself.

'I can't imagine where you were expecting to find that kind of strength,' he says, breaking the awkward silence. 'After helping Jack, you've been struggling to even stand upright.'

Max knows he's right. She'll need at least a few days to recover from yesterday's ordeal.

'You need to rest. How about you stay here while I go find us some food.'

What! She looks at him, hoping he's joking.

He lowers himself to the ground. 'You'll be okay. Just pull up the rope once I'm down,' he calls. 'I won't be long … promise.'

And just like that, he's gone.

You've got to be kidding me!

She's suddenly all alone in the forest, not knowing what dangers could be lurking out there. Her heart starts to race as her breathing accelerates. She lies down, trying to remain inconspicuous. Her ears strain to listen for anything that might be a threat. The sound of an innocent bird nearby makes her jump. She grabs the hessian sack that's lying there and throws it over herself, hoping to hide from view.

And then she starts praying that Ryker keeps his word and comes back quickly.

5

Whoa!

Ryker

Ryker stands on a large rock and catches a few fish from the stream with his trusted spear. He smiles as he thinks of Max and her stubborn independence. He likes that in a girl. But what he likes more is seeing her passion, seeing her eyes light up with excitement knowing that she can make a difference here. His heart swells knowing that he's helping her do this.

Having caught enough fish, Ryker prepares to build a small fire to cook their meal. He gathers up bits of twigs and bark to use as tinder and kindling, then goes about getting the fire started by rubbing his hands rapidly up and down a stick used as a spindle, to create the friction required. Soon the delicious aroma of the cooked fish draws the attention of his new acquaintance, Medwin.

'It's good to see you, my friend. Come and join me.'

'Although I had foreseen it,' the small man begins, 'I am still a little astonished to see you here.'

'I can tell you, it wasn't easy. We had a battle on our hands, that's for sure,' Ryker tells him. 'Most managed to get away, but two of us remain. Our friends will be coming back for us soon, and we need to be ready for them. So, Medwin, if any of you want to come with us, you need to be prepared. Can you spread the word?'

'Many are weak and too frail to travel,' Medwin says. 'And there are some who fear the unknown and are reluctant to leave. They trust me, but question my unorthodox choices. Perhaps they will listen to you if you talk to them and tell them about the place you come from.'

Ryker considers his situation. Max is too frail at the moment to deal with anything like this. 'How about we meet again here in two days. Have your people come, and I'll talk to them. I've got to go now because I need to get back to my friend.'

He hands his new friend some fish to cook for himself. In return, Medwin offers him a small sack of dried dates and berries. 'You have been good to me, Ryker, please accept this as a token of my appreciation. I will look forward to our meeting, until then, keep safe.'

Ryker is anxious to get back to Max. He's taken longer than he expected to. With his fish wrapped securely in some large leaves, he takes off into the forest and doesn't stop running until he reaches the treehouse.

Out of breath, he calls up to her, 'Hey, Max, I'm back. Sorry I took so long. Throw down the rope.' He waits a moment, but gets no response. 'Max?'

He doesn't wait another second. He dumps the food and scales up the trunk in a panic. He finds Max curled up under the hessian sacks, fast asleep. His relief is huge, but he needs a moment to compose himself. He shakes away the images that flashed before his eyes in those seconds it took him to get up there, then he lowers himself back down by rope, gathers his discarded supplies and climbs back up. Suddenly exhausted, he lies by her side and while looking up at the forest canopy decides he'll never leave her side again. He won't risk anything happening to her. He vowed to protect her, so protect her he will. Always.

They spend the next two days lying low. And true to his word, apart from the obligatory toilet break, Ryker doesn't leave Max's side.

'So do you think they're still out there looking for us?' Max asks on the second day.

Ryker rubs his temples, trying to relieve the stress there. 'It's hard to know for sure. But I trust my gut, and at the moment it's telling me to keep my guard up.'

'Yeah, I know what you mean. I'm feeling a bit iffy about things, too. It's weird; it's just too quiet, don't you think?'

Ryker smiles at her use of another Aussie term. 'I guess the word "iffy" means uncertain. Am I right?'

Max laughs at the teasing expression on his face.

He smiles at her. 'I like hearing you laugh.'

Max's face turns a deep shade of pink, and she looks away.

'I, I mean …' he stutters, looking for a way to cover his slip-up, '… it's good to see that you're feeling better.' He gives himself a mental kick.

'I'm not such a princess, you know,' she says with a pout. 'I'm pretty tough when I need to be.'

He laughs, holding up his hands in mock defence. 'Oh, I don't doubt that for a second, but don't get me wrong, you really did look like you were done for the other day, after helping Jack, I mean.' He hesitates for a moment before going on. 'Can I ask you something? And please don't take it the wrong way, but why did you do it? I mean, why did you bother removing the arrow?'

She shoots him an icy glare.

Ryker instantly regrets his words. His hands jerk back up in front of him. 'Hey, whoa, I was just asking!'

Max's stare makes him shift uncomfortably.

He needs to look away. 'Man, that death stare's a weapon,' he mumbles to himself. He dares to look back at her and sees that she's not impressed, not by a long shot. 'Okay, this is all coming out wrong.' He tries again. 'I mean, I know *why* you did it, but I was thinking, wouldn't it have been safer to have left it until he got medical help?'

Max's expression grows even more hostile. Her nostrils flare, and the crease between her brows furrows even deeper. 'What do you think I was doing? Playing Scrabble? I thought I *was* giving him medical help!'

'Hey, back up a sec. This is by no means a personal attack. I meant to say, until we got him to a hospital.'

That stops her short. Her composure changes, and she looks away, rattled by his argument. He watches as she struggles to answer.

Her shoulders suddenly slump over, and she looks down at her feet, defeated. She slowly lets out a deep breath. 'I'm sorry. You're right. Normally it would've been safer to leave it,' she admits softly.

She looks up at him with tear filled eyes, all the fire gone from the fight. 'I was planning to patch him up initially. You know, just enough to get him through to the other side. But when I saw how dangerously close the arrowhead was to puncturing a vital blood vessel, I couldn't leave it.' Max chokes back her tears. 'Any pressure on that artery would've killed him—and I'm not kidding; it was that close. A bump the wrong way and he would've died.'

She turns away, clearly battling with her emotions, and discretely wipes away the moisture on her cheeks. 'I know that by making that decision, I stuffed up our escape, and I'm sorry. But if I had to do it again, I swear I wouldn't change a thing.'

Ryker's heart sinks a little. He can see the love she has for Jack, and deep down inside the reality of it hurts. 'You know something,' he tells her, 'Jack is a bloody lucky guy, and I hope he realises it.'

'Yeah.' She blows out a controlled breath. 'It was touch and go for a moment there. But I think I did enough.'

Ryker smiles at her misunderstanding. 'He means a lot to you, doesn't he?'

Once again the colour rises up her neck to flush her face. 'I would've done the same for anyone,' she protests.

'I know you would've, but with Jack it's different

… anyone can see that.'

She squirms a little more. 'He's my friend, Ryker. I couldn't handle anything happening to him, or to any of my friends.' She remains quiet for a long while, deep in her own thoughts.

He doesn't press her further.

'I guess you'd understand, if you knew me better,' she says eventually. 'Next to Annie, he's the best person I know.'

'Who's Annie?'

Max's face lights up at the mention of her name. 'Annie's my best friend. Well, she's more than that really. She's like my surrogate mum.'

This gets his attention.

'You see,' she says hesitantly, 'my own mum died three years ago, and Annie was there, and has always been there really, to pick up the pieces.'

'Wow, I'm sorry, Max. Sounds like you've had it tough,' he says, his mind painting a clearer picture of the person in front of him. He knows how devastated he'd be if one of his parents died. 'So Annie's your father's partner now?'

She chuckles. 'No way! Annie's old enough to be my grandmother.'

Ryker can't make heads or tails of it. 'I'm lost …'

Max explains who Annie is.

Ryker smiles as he watches her talk. He can see

the love she has for her friend. 'She sounds amazing. What about your dad, you must really miss him.'

Max stiffens, and her smile vanishes.

This sudden change surprises him. Ryker misses his father more than he can say, so he's stumped to understand her reaction. He waits to hear about him, but she says nothing. 'So what does he do?' he prompts.

'He's a doctor,' she says coolly.

'That kind of makes sense, you being a healer and all.' Ryker waits for more, but Max has clammed up. 'That's it?'

'Look, I really don't want to talk about him.'

Okay, now that's weird!

Seeing that they've come to an abrupt halt in this particular discussion, he changes the topic. 'So are you feeling okay about meeting Medwin later? I'd go by myself, but I don't want to leave you on your own.'

Max stares at him with her brow once again knit in anger. 'Why would you go without me?'

Man, I can't catch a break! Somehow, he's upset her again.

'Come on, Max, it's not safe. I've got no idea who'll turn up at this gathering. Medwin, I feel I can trust, but anyone else … well, I don't know what to expect.'

'I'm not a china doll, Ryker, so stop wrapping

me up in cotton wool!'

Whoa! Once again he sees that he needs to back off a bit. Max is clearly offended by his overprotectiveness. Maybe she's not as fragile as he first thought she was.

'Hey, look, I'm sorry,' she adds. 'I appreciate what you're doing, really I do, but like it or not, we're in this together, okay? We need to help these people, and convince them to come back with us.' Her eyes plead with him. 'It's just so wrong what The Ancients are doing. These people are suffering, and all for their own selfish amusement.'

Ryker can see how passionate she is to bring about this change, and it reminds him that it was her idea to help them in the first place. 'I'm sorry. I can see that in trying to protect you, I've offended you. I get it. I know this was going to be your fight, and, as usual, I've bullied my way in taking over.'

A crooked smile appears on her face, reassuring him. 'Ryker, your heart's in the right place, I can see that, but don't shut me out. Let's do this thing together, okay?'

Ryker pulls Max into a big bear hug. 'Hey, no more cotton wool; I promise, okay?' he laughs and gives her a little peck on the top of her head. 'So we're good?'

Max squeezes him back and smiles. 'Yeah, we're good … you big, over-protective, bully.'

6

And Now We Wait

Jack sits quietly with the others, hidden in the underbrush of the forest, praying that Peanut and Kenny return quickly with help. He's got a clear view of the portal and doesn't allow himself to deviate from the task of its surveillance. But the gossamer veil remains tranquil, floating in front of him without a hint of any activity to indicate Max's return.

Thankfully there's been no sign of the portal guards returning. They're out there somewhere, but at the moment they're not his priority. Max is.

'They've been gone a while,' Banji says to him. 'Do you think they'll find anyone?'

Jack snaps out of his deep train of thought and

takes a moment to regroup his thinking. He hadn't realised Peanut and Kenny had been gone so long. And now Banji's concern has him worried. His own reservations come to a head, but he keeps them to himself.

'Don't worry, Banj, I remember when some kids vanished from here a few years ago,' he tells him, 'there was a huge search party out scouring the place for weeks, maybe even months—I can't remember exactly—but it had pretty intense media coverage for ages, anyway. So I reckon there's someone out there looking for us right now.'

'These kids you're talking about, would they be the ones we battled four years ago? Max seemed to think so.'

'She told you this?'

Banji looks away, suddenly uncomfortable. 'Well, she didn't actually tell me; I kind of read her mind that time Ryker took her.'

Jack stiffens at the reminder. Suddenly he envisages, quite clearly, the torment Max had to endure that day.

'Jack, I know what you're thinking, and I get how this must look, but I promise you, none of us had any idea what Ryker was planning back then. If we had, we would've stopped him.'

Jack looks at him from out of the corner of his

eye.

'As it was, we were lucky to talk him out of doing what he threatened to do to her.'

'What the hell was he going to do?' Jack jumps up, furious with this revelation, and immediately regrets it. He keels over from the pain in his side.

Banji holds his hands up, regret in his expression. 'Hey, I'm sorry; I didn't mean to freak you out. God, this is all coming out wrong. We weren't going to let anything happen to Max, I swear.' He then helps Jack to sit back on a fallen tree trunk.

Jack presses his palms into his eye sockets, trying to ward off his escalating rage.

Banji tries again. 'Listen, Ryker isn't that person anymore. He wasn't that guy when we first entered the Realm, and he's definitely not that person now. What we suffered over the years created that monster, and believe me when I tell you, that monster thankfully died in that tragic chariot race.'

Jack gives himself few minutes to let that sink in. He needs to believe Banji is telling him the truth, that Max is safe with him in there.

The sound of movement at the top of the ravine has their immediate attention. Jack looks up, shielding his eyes from the glare of the sun, and sees Peanut and his famous lopsided grin. And right behind him comes Kenny and an army of men and women, mostly in tactical gear.

They're finally safe.

One of the men pushes past Peanut with sudden urgency and stops abruptly to survey the bottom of the ravine. Jack's heart stops—it's his dad.

'Jack!' His father scrambles down the slope, almost toppling over in his desperation to get to him.

'Dad!' Tears prick at Jack's eyes. He races towards him, but a sharp pain reminds him of his injury. He stops, bent over, clutching at his side.

'Good God, you're hurt!'

Daniel Braden closes the distance between them and has Jack wrapped in his embrace in seconds. He looks down at his son's blood-drenched shirt, then calls out in a panic for medical assistance.

An army of support—police personnel, soldiers and paramedics—rapidly descend the slope. There's sudden pandemonium as they each radio back to their respective bases.

The sound of a helicopter overhead makes Jack anxious about what's going to happen next. 'Dad, we've got to go back. Max and Ryker are still there. They need our help.'

'Son, let the right people take care of that. Let's focus on getting you to safety.'

'But you don't understand; we can't go yet!'

Two paramedics lay a stretcher on the ground

next to him, and his protests fall on deaf ears as they start to examine his injuries. They cuff his arm to assess his blood pressure, flash a light in his eyes and bombard him with a million and one questions—questions he knows are only delaying Max's rescue.

Caught in the confusion, he struggles to explain to his father, and anyone who'll listen, what needs to be done—urgently. 'Dad, I'm okay, really. Please, we've got to go back.'

One of the paramedics pulls up Jack's shirt to examine his wound. His father gasps at the sight of it.

'Buddy, you're not in any condition to go anywhere but straight to the nearest hospital.' The paramedic has the final say on the matter, ending any hope, there and then, that they'll act on Jack's appeal.

An official-looking man approaches him. 'Jack, you said we need to go back - back where, son? Where have you all been? And where exactly are these other two kids you're referring to?'

Unable to talk freely because of the oxygen mask that's been placed over his mouth and nose, Jack points to the transparent, wispy veil behind him. The man turns to the portal, studies it for a good while, scratches his head, then turns back to Jack. 'What? Through there?'

Jack nods.

'It's a portal to another dimension,' Kenny says as

he approaches.

'It's true. We've been trapped in there,' Jack tries to tell them.

The official stares at Jack, then Kenny, as if they're both talking in a foreign language. He then picks a broken branch off the ground, turns it in his hand a few times, appearing to be in two minds as to his next move, and then, with his decision apparently made, tosses it through the gossamer curtain.

The branch vanishes before their eyes.

With a look of complete and utter disbelief on his face, he turns to Jack's father for validation on what he'd just witnessed.

Jack's dad stands up, his eyes wide with alarm. The men look at each other in bewilderment. Others also see this inexplicable phenomenon, and a crowd forms around them. For a good few seconds, no one utters a single word.

'I, I … I've never seen anything like it.' The official shakes his head as he struggles to make sense of it. And then, just like a flick of a switch, his mind snaps back to the situation at hand, and he reverts to calling out orders and instructions. 'Daniel, we'll have Jack airlifted to hospital as soon as they've stabilised him. The terrain is too unpredictable to do it any other way.'

This reminds Jack's father of Jack's injury. 'I'm

grateful, Captain Logan,' he says. 'How are the other kids?' He looks around at the remaining children. 'Dear God, Dean,' he says, horrified, 'we need to get these kids back to their families as soon as possible.'

Jack looks at his friends and takes in their appearance as though seeing them through his father's eyes. To his alarm, they look almost barbaric. The sight of Edra, Ulan and Banji, in particular, with their dirty faces, undernourished frames and threadbare clothes, is suddenly very disturbing. How hadn't he noticed that before?

'Come on, son, let's get you home.'

7

ꟻAMOUS

Daniel Braden gets up from the visitor's chair in the hospital ward. 'I'm just going to step outside to make a phone call. Can I get you boys anything? I'm getting a coffee for myself …'

Jack shakes his head. His father hasn't left his side since they were found. 'Dad, you need to get some sleep. Go home, I'll be okay.'

'So that'll be nothing for you, then?' he winks at him. 'Peanut, anything? They've got some chocolate glazed doughnuts at the cafeteria …'

'We're good, Mr B. Thanks anyway.'

Jack's father frowns slightly and hesitates a moment longer than necessary before leaving, as if puzzled by the turn-down.

Jack lets out a deep sigh. He's worried about him.

'Hey, the nightly news is about to come on,' Peanut announces, eyes gleaming with excitement. He plonks himself on the bed next to Jack. 'I wonder if they're gonna talk about us again.'

Jack laughs at his best friend's obsession with their sudden catapult to fame.

'And can you believe it? They haven't been able to track down those guards yet. Go figure. Surely it can't be that hard to find them? They're the size of two small elephants, for crying out loud!'

Jack looks at him and laughs.

'Anyway, it's a bit of a worry is all I'm saying … you know, with those goons running amok out there. I wonder if there's been an update on that. Hey, shut up, it's about to start.'

'News Headline… Police are still on the lookout for two armed and dangerous men last seen in the Blue Ridge National Park on the southern coast of New South Wales. The pair reportedly were involved in the kidnapping of the five children that went missing last month while on a school camp. They are described as being approximately one-hundred-and-eighty, to two-hundred centimetres tall, each weighing approximately one-hundred-and-fifty kilograms. The public are warned to stay away from this area and to immediately report

anything suspicious to the police.

'Today I have with me in the studio the ASIO spokesperson in charge of the investigation, Deputy Director General Gerard Thompson.'

The reporter then directs the interview to an Official sitting at the desk.

'Thank you for joining us today, Deputy Director General. Now, there's been speculation as to the origin of these two men, and we can assume, because of ASIO's involvement, that these men pose a threat to our national security, but are you able to disclose the nature of this threat?'

'At this stage, no.'

'Can we presume that they're terrorists?'

'Terrorists? Where did that come from?' Peanut shakes his head, incredulous.

'No, that's not true. The assailants in question are indirectly involved in the disappearance of the five teenagers.'

The photos of each of the missing persons in question appear on the screen, including Max's.

Jack's stomach clenches.

'Hey, there we are again!' Peanut cries out.

'Then can you explain ASIO's involvement? Are we looking at an international child trafficking racket? Our source tells us that another three teenagers were amongst those children found, a boy and two girls from South

Africa.'

'I'm not at liberty to comment on that at this stage. The persons in question are all currently being attended to, and are, for the most part, unharmed.'

The reporter continues questioning the official regarding what the public need to do to assist in detaining the offenders.

'Told ya we'd be famous, didn't I?' Peanut laughs.

Kenny and Ruby run into the room. 'Hey, did you catch the news?' Ruby asks with excitement.

'Yeah, you looked pretty hot there, Rubes,' Peanut teases. 'So where are the others? Are they coming?'

'The doctors are checking them out still. Listen,' she says, lowering her voice, 'I'm a bit worried about Edra. I don't think she's doing so well. You know that guy that died—Jaeger—well, she's in a real mess having to relive what happened to him for the police report. Poor thing, it must be so hard for her.'

Jack doesn't want to voice it, but he's in a whole world of pain, too, not knowing what's happening to Max. *Is she safe? Did Ryker manage to get them away in time? Or has she been caught? Has she been tortured? Is she even still alive!*

'Mate, you don't look so good all of a sudden,' Peanut tells him, his concern obvious. 'How about I call the nurse?'

'I'm okay.' He quickly diverts the attention. 'So

what do you reckon has happened to Max and Ryker? Do you think they got away? Those thugs wouldn't have come after us if they had the chance to go after them, right?'

'Mate, quit beating yourself up. You've asked us that a million times already—you know that, right?' Peanut looks at him a little closer. 'Are you sure you didn't hit your head in that fall? I swear you've got concussion.'

Kenny nudges him. 'Leave him alone, Peanut. Yeah, Jack, you've got a point; they wouldn't have come after us if Max and Ryker were still there. Maybe they're—'

A knock at the door interrupts the conversation. A woman in a smart, tailored suit enters, holding a huge microphone in her hand. A cameraman accompanies her. 'Hi there, my name is Trina Portabella, reporting for Channel 8 News,' she says with a plastic smile. 'So you're the kids that were abducted by the child traffickers. Our sources tell us that two other teenagers are still being held by them, one of which is the daughter of wealthy Professor Edward Rutherford. Can you tell me, do you think this is an extortion attempt?'

She places the offensive microphone in front of Ruby, who's clearly shocked speechless by the intrusion. The reporter waits to hear her response.

Jack jumps out of the bed and smacks it away. 'Get out of here! Who let you in, anyway?'

'Jack, is it?' the reporter continues. 'Can you tell us where you've all been held hostage these last few weeks? Are there more captives, apart from the two mentioned, that we don't know about? Tell us how you got away.'

Jack reaches for the red emergency button on the wall, setting off an alarm. The effort makes him double over in pain.

'Can you tell us what conditions you were kept in?' the reporter continues. 'You're obviously in a lot of pain. Did they hurt you? I've heard that one of the kids held there died. Can you elaborate on that? Are they torturing innocent children?'

A nurse runs into the ward and calls out for security when she realises what's happening.

The reporter raises her voice. 'The public have a right to know exactly what's going on here! Who's behind this child-trafficking racket? Are our children safe?'

Security arrive within seconds and manage to clear the room after a very heated altercation and a few choice threats involving the police.

'Man, that was heavy. Rubes, are you okay?' Peanut puts his arm around her. She looks a little rattled by the assault.

'Can you believe the stuff she was coming up with?' Kenny says, gobsmacked. 'Remind me not to trust everything they tell us on the news.'

'She must've been listening at the door,' Jack realises. 'How else would she have known all that? The public reports haven't said anything about Max and Ryker, have they?'

'Or Jaeger,' Ruby reminds them.

'Mate, I take it back … I don't think being famous is everything it's cracked up to be,' Peanut says soberly.

Jack laughs without humour. 'Yeah, you can say that again.'

Later that night, while Jack absently watches the television, breaking news disrupts the program. He rolls his eyes in disgust and turns it off.

8

Get A Grip

It's eerily cold and dark. Jack rubs his arms to stir up some heat. He stands hidden, at a safe distance, watching the gauzy veil floating tranquilly in front of him … teasing … beckoning him to enter.

And then there's a change. The portal begins to quiver with excited energy. For a split second, he thinks he sees Max. But in that instant, he can't be sure, and she's already gone again.

He rubs at his eyes and races towards the portal, shouting out her name.

The curtain continues to oscillate with life. He sees her struggling to pass again, but she can't— something's pulling at her, holding her back. One second she's there, the next she's gone. Try as she might, she can't get through. As quickly as she materialises, she disappears, hauled back into the nothingness, and lost to him.

He has to find a way to go to her. She needs him. *Max!*

He cries out, but no sound escapes him to be heard.

Once again she emerges, but to his horror, she's drenched in blood. He tries to reach out to her, but something drags him away. He fights against the invisible restraints, but to no avail. His feet are like lead weights, weighed down so heavily that he can't move them. The harder he fights to get to her, the slower his progress.

Max! Max!

But his cries are drowned out by the white noise that deafens him.

Frantic, he reaches out for her again, but the portal gets further and further away. And then, suddenly, it vanishes.

Jack sits upright in a sweat. The abrupt movement sends a stabbing pain to his side. His heart is racing, his breathing erratic. He looks around, disorientated until he sees his father asleep in the hospital armchair next to his bed. He takes a moment to calm himself, but the knot in his stomach is hard to ignore.

It's dark outside and difficult to tell what time it is. He gazes out the window, trying to suppress the images still fresh in his mind's eye. He won't be able to go back to sleep again after that nightmare. Not that it makes a difference. He hasn't been able to sleep well since being back. His concern for Max consumes him. His first thoughts when he wakes are about her.

Who's he kidding? His every tortured thought is about her. An overwhelming anxiety hits him like a ton of bricks each time he relives those last crucial moments—when he left her behind. The guilt is killing him.

He pulls at his hair in frustration. *I've got to stop doing this. I'm useless to her if I keep falling apart every time my head goes there.*

What he needs is to talk to someone. He throws off his blanket and is about to sneak out to visit Peanut in the room next door when he remembers that he, Ruby and Kenny were discharged earlier that day. Reluctantly he lays back down and stares blankly at the ceiling.

But his mind starts to race again, and soon he becomes unbearably agitated. He looks hopefully over at his father, then sighs. His dad isn't the one that'll reassure him.

He then remembers Edra and the twins.

Carefully, he slips out of bed and makes his way

down the corridor to their room. By the time he gets there, the pain in his side has lessened. He stands at the doorway looking in. The darkness in the room makes it hard to tell whether anyone's awake.

'Jack?' a croaky voice calls out from the bed nearest the window. 'Can't sleep, huh?' Banji sits up and rubs the sleep out of his eyes.

'Nah, you?'

'On and off. I keep waking up in a sweat thinking that we're still there.'

Knowing he's not the only one consoles Jack. 'Hey, aren't your olds flying in today?'

'Yeah, I can hardly believe it.' Banji pulls himself up and fixes his pillows. 'Maybe it'll feel real when I finally see them. Talking over the phone just isn't the same.'

They sit in a comfortable silence.

'You know it kills me knowing what they've been through, losing both of us like that.' Banji gets too choked up to go on. Tears pool in his eyes, and he turns away to discretely swipe at them.

Jack struggles hearing this. He can't even begin to imagine their suffering.

'In a way, I've kind of been lucky,' Banji says on reflection, 'at least I've had Ulan with me the whole time. Family's everything, you know. And I guess now, with what we've all been through, you could say that Ryker and Edra are family, too.'

'I heard you guys lost a friend in the final challenge. That must've been tough.'

'Yeah, Jaeger. His parents are coming, too. I guess they need some kind of closure,' he says quietly. 'God, I'm dreading that. His death was the hardest thing I've ever gone through.' He remains silent for a few moments, clearly struggling with those memories.

'I'm sorry, Banj.'

Banji clears his throat and shakes his head. 'Did you know, Jae and I were best friends. Our families have known each other for years. It'll be hard for them, seeing us and knowing that he'll never be coming home.'

Jack fights to handle his emotions.

'And I'll tell you right now, Edra won't cope with any of it.' He turns to look at the bed nearest the door. 'That day he died, she completely fell apart. It took her forever to deal with it. And having to relive it again now,' he says, pulling at his hair uneasily, 'well, let's just say that it'll be a long time before she gets back on track.'

They both look at Edra, who's sleeping peacefully.

'They've had to sedate her just so her body can rest. She's been a mess since she heard that his parents were on their way. But she's got us, and her parents are coming, so we'll get through this together.'

'I hear Ryker's parents are coming, too.'

'Now that'll be interesting,' Banji suddenly laughs.

His reaction surprises Jack.

'Yeah, Ryker's dad's a big-wig in the South African Navy. He was actually in the marine corps when it was still functioning during the apartheid era. Vice Admiral Denvon Engelbrecht. I tell you, be prepared, because he's a force to be reckoned with.'

Jack's eyes pop wide open.

'You'll see what I mean when you meet him. Ryker's their only child, so I'll guarantee that things won't be quiet when he gets here. Knowing him, he'll march through those doors with a plan of action already in place. The Ancients won't know what hit them. What I would give to be a fly on the wall when that happens.'

Jack smirks. He can picture Ryker's dad, bold as brass, terrorising the nobles of the Ancient Realm.

Talking to Banji has lifted his spirits somewhat. But in no time his thoughts go back to Max. He wonders why her father hasn't come to the hospital to see them—not that he should care for any of them, after all he doesn't know them, but both of Ryker's parents are flying in to be here, so why can't he make some kind of effort?

Jack's heart breaks a little, knowing there's no one

coming for her.

'Hey, what's made you so angry all of a sudden?'

Only then does Jack realise he's gritting his teeth. He gets up from Banji's bed and starts to pace. He can't get his head around it. He knows Max and her father have a fractured relationship, but he would think that he'd at least try to find out first-hand what happened. Any parent would. His anger escalates. 'Do you really want to know what I'm thinking? We haven't heard a thing from Max's dad, no phone call, no visit, no nothing. Just where the hell is he? Why hasn't he bothered to come?'

Banji shrugs. 'I suppose he's spoken to the police already, and read our statements. Maybe he can't deal with seeing us safely home while she's still missing.'

He's not buying it. Jack's not going to let him off that easy. But that's not Banji's fault, and Jack quickly realises it. 'Sorry, mate, I'm just worried about them, that's all.'

'I know you are. We all are. But what you need to do is keep reminding yourself that Max is with Ryker. He'll never let anything happen to her.'

Wow, now that didn't help one bit like it should've!

Jack's heart rate suddenly triples. He tries not to overreact. He takes a few deep, calming breathes to quash his jealousy. He's an emotional mess, and he knows it. What he needs to do is to get out of there, and fast. 'Thanks, buddy. Look, I'm gonna try to get some sleep. You should too.' And before Banji has a chance to say anything, Jack makes his escape.

Man, I've really gotta get my shit together!

9

The Trade-Off

Max

Mid-afternoon, Max and Ryker descend from the treehouse and make their way toward the stream. Max stays as close to Ryker as possible, her earlier bravado suddenly questionable. She watches him as he paves the way looking everywhere and responding to every forest sound. She, too, has her senses piqued. Her adrenalin- induced, high-alert mode has her ready to run.

Once they reach the stream, she finds that she's already totally exhausted because of it. But the sound of the flowing water revitalises her. She's so desperate to bathe, she jumps in without a second thought.

After the initial shock of the cool water, she starts

to revel in the first opportunity in days for a thorough wash. She's in heaven. She could very easily spend an hour lazing in the refreshing water but is conscious that they'll soon be meeting with the forest people. She scrubs at the blood stains on her clothes as best she can, not wanting to scare them off before she gets a chance to talk to them. She washes her long dark hair and wraps it up in a tight bun, then sits for a moment on a rock, drying in the late sun.

Ryker has remained vigilant the whole time. Although busy fishing, his eyes have constantly surveyed the area, prepared for anything.

The afternoon starts to dwindle, but there's no sign of them. She voices her concern. 'I wonder if they'll come.'

But before he can reply, a nearby rustling tells them that someone's approaching. Max jumps to her feet, and Ryker moves to her side.

A small man carrying a spear appears in the clearing. He has long, dark hair, a short, scraggly beard and wears a hessian sack. Ryker walks towards him with his hand extended. The small man hesitantly offers his hand, and his face lights up with a friendly smile. Max relaxes and watches the exchange.

This must be Medwin.

Ryker towers over the smaller man. 'Hello, my friend; have you come alone?'

'Many are here, but remain concealed.' He studies Max, his eyes narrowed in caution. 'Who have you here?'

Ryker makes the introductions. 'It's because of Max's foresight and determination that we're attempting to do this.'

'So this is she!' Medwin looks at her, surprised. 'Such big ideas for such a small person.'

Max smiles at their new friend. He doesn't stand that much taller than herself. 'We'd like to help you if we can,' she begins nervously, then turns to Ryker who gives her an encouraging wink. 'We want to take you back with us. We come from a place where there's plenty of food and shelter. And we have people that can heal the sick and protect the young.' Max tries to sound convincing without laying it on too thick.

'So tell me,' Ryker asks, 'are there many of you interested in leaving?'

'You have healers?' Medwin interrupts, his interest piqued. 'There are many of us that are maimed or ill. Can your healers help us?'

Ryker, in his excitement, reveals that Max is a healer, and that she saved his life in the chariot challenge. 'My skull was crushed by the horses, and I died. Max brought me back to life.'

'Surely not! I cannot believe this,' Medwin's eyes grow wide, genuinely astounded.

Max sees a perfect opportunity to gain their trust. 'You said that some of you are unwell; bring them here and I can show you what I can do.'

Medwin looks at her for a while with scepticism, then turns to the forest and calls out to one of the forest dwellers. 'Alger, come forth.'

A tall, thin man appears tentatively from the bushes nursing an arm that juts out at an unnatural angle.

'Once our village had two hunters: Molan, our chief provider, and Alger,' Medwin explains. 'Molan was maimed two years ago and is now lame. As a result, our dependence on Alger had become vital. But recently he injured his arm. As you can imagine, our village is suffering. Food is becoming scarce. If not for the generosity Ryker has shown us, we would be experiencing a terrible hardship.'

'Will you let me have a look? I think I can help,' Max asks the hesitant man.

Alger turns to Medwin, his eyes showing his panic, but the smaller man reassures him with a nod.

Max knows she can do this—she's done it before—but the butterflies fluttering in her stomach make her stupidly doubt herself. Trying to ignore the pressure she's put on herself, she reaches out and carefully places her hands on his broken arm. The hunter, clearly a reluctant volunteer, closes his eyes tight, but allows her to proceed.

The familiar heat begins to generate in her core, then starts to radiate to her fingertips. Alger jerks his arm away in fright and turns once again to Medwin, silently pleading for his reassurance.

'The heat you're feeling will heal you,' Ryker says. 'Trust it.'

Medwin places a supportive hand on Alger and gestures for Max to go on.

She readily continues—this might be the turning point they need in this new alliance—and before long, the watchers witness the repair of the hunter's broken arm.

Alger's eyes open and widen when he sees the result. He turns to his friend, at a loss for words.

Medwin wears an identical expression of amazement. 'How can this be?'

The bushes around them rustle, and several people reveal themselves, keen to witness the result of the healing.

Alger cautiously tests his arm. 'What power is this? I am healed!' He raises his arm for all to see.

The crowd gasps.

More and more people come forward. Soon, Max and Ryker are surrounded by so many that it's difficult to estimate numbers.

'Like I said,' Max says, excited at the reaction,

'where we come from, we have people that help the sick. Come back with us.' But in saying this, Max feels she needs to make something clear. 'We can't fix things the way you just saw me do it. Don't get me wrong, we still can, just differently, and the healing takes time. My ability to heal like this is something I got only when I came here.'

'Wait. Let me understand this, for it is pivotal,' Medwin interrupts, suddenly looking very concerned. 'Is it your meaning that we may lose our special powers when we cross into your world?'

His question silences the rowdy crowd.

'I have the gift of intuition,' he continues, 'and it is with this skill that has allowed me and my family to remain safe in the forest. If I was to leave the forest, will I be sacrificing this?'

Max realises that this could be a deal breaker. She turns to Ryker for help.

After some hesitation, Ryker answers. 'This could be the case; we've no way of knowing until we actually pass through the gateway.'

Alarm spreads amongst the forest people.

'Listen, we can't be sure about anything,' Max calls out. 'Please, just hear me out.'

'Let the healer have her say,' Medwin shouts over the throng of panic.

The crowd immediately becomes silent.

'Thank you,' Max begins. 'I can only tell you from what I've seen, and that is, when a person passes through to your world, their natural ability intensifies. For example, normally, Ryker is physically strong, but his strength here is magnified. Can you see what I'm trying to say? You won't lose your given abilities, they'll be less powerful, that's all.'

This stirs the crowd to break into anxious private conversations again.

Her enthusiasm takes a nose-dive. She looks at Ryker. 'Something tells me that didn't go down too well.'

'Don't beat yourself up; you had to tell them.'

'Then answer me this,' someone calls from the crowd, 'what will we gain from leaving our homes and coming with you?'

The crowd become increasingly rowdy, clearly needing to hear the answer.

Ryker tries to calm them. 'We can promise you a better life. I've been held here against my will for four years. I've experienced torture, hunger and suffering. I've witnessed death. I'm fighting to escape this place because I know what lies beyond. The fortress has been left in ruins - if you think you've had hardship up until now, then realise this, there will be more suffering - The Ancients will retaliate. Please, let us help you. Our friends will be returning any day now to help those of you who want to come back with us.'

Max looks into the silent crowd and can see that his speech has made an impact. Hell, it very nearly brought a tear to her own eye.

Ryker turns to leave, but before they go, Max has an idea. 'Look, I get it that some of you are afraid to come—that's okay; you don't have to—but give me a chance to help you anyway. Come back tomorrow, and I'll heal anyone who needs it.'

Ryker takes her hand and squeezes it. 'Well done, you. Maybe they'll think a little differently now.'

She winks at him. 'That's the plan.'

They travel silently back through the forest, Max deep in thought, hoping that enough was said to make the forest people want to leave. *Why would they choose to stay here? Surely, it's a no-brainer.*

But could it be a different type of cruelty to take them away from the only life they know? She takes a moment to consider this. Ryker had told her that most of them have lived their whole lives in the forest. Medwin himself is a second-generation forest dweller, never having known anything but the forest as his home.

All these questions so fill Max's head that she doesn't notice a large figure appear before them from the shadows and swing a huge tree branch straight at Ryker's head. Before either of them has had time to react, Ryker falls to the ground. Blood gushes from the wound, and his body convulses briefly before suddenly going limp.

Max looks down at his lifeless body in horror. She can't breathe. *He's dead!*

But her fight instinct snaps her back to what she needs to do. She looks around for something with which to defend herself. Seeing nothing, she turns and makes a run for it back down the path, hoping to find someone who can help. The adrenalin in her veins spurs her on, her chaser sounding close behind. She ducks and weaves through the bushes, her arms and legs gashed and whipped as she pushes through denser vegetation. In a panic she realises that she's come off the path and is now ensnared by the forest, cornered, and up for the taking.

She turns to see her pursuer standing before her, breathless from the run, but he smiles at her predicament. 'Your capture will fetch me a healthy reward, healer. Now be a good lass and give in to me.'

Max frantically searches for an escape route, but she's well and truly trapped.

All she can do now is hope that Medwin is nearby to hear her. She screams for help. But the stranger grabs her, muzzles her mouth with his filthy hand, muting her attempts, and restrains her movements with his massive frame. She fights and squirms, trying to weaken his hold, and kicks and bites at the hand clawing at her mouth.

But her abductor won't have any of that. He slams her up against a tree, winding her into silence, then leans into her—his face inches away—and leers menacingly into her eyes. 'Try that again and I swear I will break your neck!' His spit sprays her face.

Max stares into the depth of the darkness of his soul and knows that he means every word of it.

He then stuffs a dirty rag into her mouth to keep her quiet while he ties her wrists behind her back. The smell and taste of the rag makes Max gag. Struggling to calm herself, she fights to stop from throwing up and choking on her vomit.

But, no, she won't give in. She thrashes about and calls out against the gag. Her captor yanks painfully at her arms—his patience clearly wearing thin. Tears sting her eyes from the excruciating pain. He swings her around to face him and smacks her hard across the face, finally silencing Max into submission.

He immediately hoists her over his shoulder like a sack of potatoes and makes his escape.

There's no hope; she's done for. She closes her eyes, but the image of Ryker's dead body burns on her retinas and slashes at her heart. Tears once again prickle at her senses. He's gone. She can do nothing now but say a silent goodbye to him and pray for a miracle for herself.

10

Ten Pieces Of Gold

Max

Max's abductor sets a relentless pace, and his ruthless manner as he makes his escape leaves her battered and bruised all over. Finally, they reach his destination—the fortress. Her stomach clenches knowing that the outcome of this trade-off won't end well.

At the foot of the lowered bridge, the kidnapper makes his demands. 'I want my reward before I hand her to you.'

Herodus appears at the other end of the bridge and calls back, 'You are not in a position for ultimatums, Slade, you piece of filth!' He motions for the guards to seize the man.

Slade realises his mistake too late. He throws Max into the path of the guards and tries to escape, but within seconds they've tackled him to the ground. There's no way out for him now. 'You promised me ten pieces of gold!' he shouts.

Herodus walks up to the captive, looks down at him and sneers. 'I lied.'

The guards yank him to his feet. Slade curses and thrashes about, struggling to break free.

'You savage!' Herodus strikes him across the face. 'This catastrophe you see before you has claimed the life of Beowulf already, and our Ancient Leader is at this very moment dying, and you think to profit from this knowledge! You disgust me. Take him away.'

The guards drag Slade away. He kicks out at them and screams, 'You will regret your actions! Mark my words, for I know what is coming, I have heard their plans.'

Max notices that his words pique Herodus' attention. His keen eye follows the prisoner as the guards drag him away. She starts to panic. If Herodus finds out what was said at the meeting, her friends' safety will be at risk. Somehow, she needs to warn them.

With slow deliberation, Herodus turns to Max, his penetrating gaze searching for those hidden secrets to which Slade alluded.

'So your friends have abandoned you? I should kill you for the devastation you have left us in. But I have a greater use for you.' He slowly runs his repulsive finger down the side of her face. If it wasn't for that gag, and if she could muster enough saliva in her parched mouth, she'd spit in his disgusting face.

'Pius is on his death bed as we speak,' he informs her. 'The elephants have mutilated his body beyond any methods of healing that we know. Your task is to save him. If by some miracle you succeed, you will somewhat redeem yourself. But if you fail, I promise you this ... the last thing you will see before your demise is the underside of the giant's foot that will crush your skull as it has our ruler's. And believe me, I will make certain that you suffer a slow and painful death.'

Max shudders at the threat. Her heart pounds out of control.

Herodus yanks the gag from her mouth, grabs Max by the scruff of the neck, and before she has had time to react, drags her away to tend to their dying ruler.

They enter a passageway off the arena which leads to an enormous hallway with doors to several rooms on either side. Everywhere Max looks, she sees a wealth of extravagance. Large, ornately carved wooden furniture adorn each room, and enormous tapestries cover the walls. Every stand soldiering the hallway displays intricate golden urns or platters embellished with precious stones.

Seeing such absurd richness on display makes her sick to the stomach, but she can't be distracted by it now. She needs to keep a lookout for a way to escape.

Herodus ushers her past several guards stationed along the impressive passageway and stops in front of an intricately carved double-door. He gives a hesitant knock. A moment later, the door opens revealing a frail-looking man with a pointed nose and oily black hair, dressed in black robes. The look on his face is one of despair.

'We are losing him, Herodus. There is nothing more I can do.'

'Eshmun, I have brought you the healer from the challenges,' Herodus says. 'She possesses advanced healing powers that we have never seen. Let her try.'

The ancient healer moves aside to allow them to enter. On a large, opulent bed, its sheets saturated with blood, lies a figure so mangled and mutilated that Max questions how the victim could still be alive. Pius's body is battered, black and blue, his skull crushed and face swollen beyond recognition.

Her heart races. *How the hell am I supposed to fix this!*

Herodus shoves her closer, urging her to start.

His threatening glare leaves her with no choice; she needs to start doing something. Instinctively she looks for some sign of life. His breathing is so shallow that she doubts her judgement. She places her hand to his throat to feel for a pulse, but the ancient healer swipes her hand away.

'I need to see if he's still alive!' she protests.

The healer looks to Herodus for guidance, and he nods his reassurance. The healer reluctantly withdraws.

Max returns to examining the patient. Once again, she places her hand on the side of the ancient ruler's neck. His pulse is critically weak. Her fingers begin to tingle, and a fierce warmth bursts from her core with an urgency that she's never felt before. The intensity of the heat makes Max momentarily pull back in alarm.

The two men jolt back, fear written on their faces.

Hesitating only to take a few calming breaths, Max proceeds. Her priority is the chest area. She senses that she'll lose him if she doesn't save his heart first. After a few minutes working there, she starts to feel the weak, irregular flutter of his heart strengthen. With the greatest relief, she moves to his crushed skull and repairs the many fractures. She senses a lot of swelling on the brain, so works to drain the fluid and ease the pressure to this delicate organ. Slowly the swelling of the tissue around his skull disappears, leaving a more recognisable person. A healthier hue replaces the black from the bruising.

Eshmun watches on in alarm. 'What kind of black magic is this?' he hisses.

Methodically and systematically, Max continues to heal a seemingly hopeless case. Crushed bones reform, and punctured organs miraculously repair. Slowly but surely their Ancient Leader returns from the dead.

But Max's energy is draining fast. She hasn't experienced exhaustion like this before. Although struggling to stay awake, she knows she can't stop now. 'Please, I need some water,' she says.

Herodus snaps out of his stunned state and quickly fills a goblet.

Max gulps it down so fast, her throat burns. 'More,' she asks, holding up the goblet with shaky hands. Thankfully she gets a refill.

She starts to feel herself regenerate, but she doesn't stop to rest. The injuries are extensive, and although appearances would indicate otherwise, Max can feel that the healing has a way to go.

Herodus starts to pace back and forth, clearly anxious to see results. 'How long do we need to wait?' he demands. 'Our Ruler appears well enough now, why has he not woken?'

Max looks down at her hands. 'My hands will let me know when the healing is done. After that, we need to give him time to rest. I don't think we'll know for sure until the morning.'

Both men exchange a worried look.

She can only imagine what they're thinking, but she can't do anything about their reservations. Time will eventually show them she's not lying. She returns to her task, and soon the heat in Max's hands dissipates, and the energy recedes from her core.

Her strength depleted, she raises her head to tell them that she has done all she can do. Stars flicker before her eyes, and a cold sweat overcomes her. The last thing she remembers is the room suddenly spinning out of control before everything goes black.

II

SLADE

RYKER

Ryker wakes disorientated with his head about to burst from excruciating pain. But he forgets all that the moment he realises Max is gone.

'Max! Max!'

Desperate to get to his feet, he staggers upright, then clutches his head as another stabbing burst of pain renders him immobile. He grabs hold of the nearest tree to help him stand before doubling over and retching the contents of his already empty stomach.

'God, please help me,' he begs as he tries to push through the pain. He wipes away the wetness blinding his vision, and his hand comes away covered in blood. He presses firmly on the wound, trying to stop the flow. Though his head spins, he forces himself to go on. He stumbles through the forest, not knowing in which direction he's going, but praying that his instincts will take him back to the stream. There he hopes to find some forest people who might be able to help him.

Medwin emerges from the woods. 'Ryker, what has happened? I had a vision that you were in need of our help.'

'We were attacked. Max is gone.'

He frowns. 'What can we do to assist?'

Suddenly several forest people appear by Medwin's side.

'Help me track her movements,' he begs.

'Of course,' Medwin says, then quickly gathers a team.

Ryker leads the small group back into the forest, retracing his steps. The trail of fresh blood enables them to move quickly. Once they reach the place where he was ambushed, they stop and survey the area, looking for any sign of Max's movements. A trail of disturbed vegetation leads them deeper into the forest until they come to where she was most likely cornered.

'There are signs of a struggle here,' Medwin says.

Ryker's heart sinks. 'She's been taken.' He searches the area for any hint as to which direction she may have gone. 'There!' He points to more disturbed vegetation. 'Let's go. They can't be too far.' Ryker runs, scouring the area for more clues as he goes. 'We're heading towards the fortress. Maybe one of the guards has her.'

'Ryker, wait!' Medwin calls. 'Alger approaches.'

The man Max healed earlier races towards them. He stops before them, and bent over, struggling to catch his breath between gasps, he tells them what he knows: 'Your healer …' he pants. 'Slade!'

'What!' Medwin cries out. 'That conspiring jackal! Ryker, this is not good.'

Ryker's blood goes cold.

'Pius is wounded …' Alger tells them between gasps. 'Slade has traded her for gold.'

Ryker staggers backwards, suddenly lightheaded. 'This can't be happening! Quick, tell me everything. We need to get to her.'

Alger catches his breath. 'I was on my way to the village when I saw Slade running towards the fortress carrying something over his shoulder. I realised it was the healer and knew he was up to no good, so I followed. At the fortress gate, he beckoned the guards to allow him to enter, for he had brought the healer to save the Ancient Leader, who is dying.'

Ryker can't believe it. There's not a second to waste. He takes off.

'You are too late,' Alger shouts after him. 'Herodus took your healer away immediately.'

Ryker stops, wavering, on the brink of collapsing. He needs to sit down.

'Herodus spoke of the death of Beowulf in the catastrophe,' Alger continues. 'And the endangering of the life of Pius. The deal has already been done.'

Ryker sinks to the ground, but his mind races, trying to figure out a way to fix this. But nothing comes to him. He cries out in frustration, 'I've got to get back in there!'

Medwin sits by his side and places a supportive hand on his shoulder. 'Listen to me; they will not harm your friend. They need her to heal the Ancient Leader; she is too valuable to them. You must remain calm and not be impetuous with your plans.'

Ryker exhales slowly, taking in Medwin's logic. 'You're right; we've got time to work this out. I need to do this right.'

'Can we delay until your friends return? They can be of assistance to you.'

Ryker contemplates this briefly but decides against it. 'No, there's no way of knowing how long they'll be. I can't risk waiting for them. I need to get in, sooner rather than later.' He remains silent for a moment, and then an idea comes to him. 'Alger, did you say that Beowulf is dead?'

'Many were killed when the elephants charged the stadium. Yes, Beowulf was one of them.'

'Does this mean it's the end to these barbaric challenges?'

Medwin shakes his head. 'I fear not. If past history has anything to go by, the arena will be rebuilt, and in no passing of time, the games will continue.'

'Is that right?'

'More than likely, yes.' Medwin considers Ryker, suspiciously. 'And what is it that has you suddenly so curious?'

'What's a challenge with only four Invincibles?' he asks.

'You are just in saying this, Ryker. Perhaps they will find another to fill Beowulf's role.'

'My point exactly. Medwin, you've hit the nail on the head.'

Medwin turns to Alger, looking baffled. 'Can you make any sense of this?'

The other man shrugs.

Ryker formulates a plan, oblivious to his friends' concerns.

'My friend, I am a little reluctant to ask, but what strategies are you scheming in that broken head of yours?'

Ryker smiles a mischievous smile. 'Just watch and learn, my friend. Just watch and learn.'

12

AELIANNA

MAX

Max stirs from her state of unconsciousness, her ears picking up on some movement nearby. She tries to move, but her body feels like a lead weight. It's an effort even to hold her eyes open long enough to investigate. She's exhausted. Through tiny slits she sees a man in black robes pacing in front of a large four-poster bed. And then the reality of her situation comes flooding back to her. Her heart pounds. She needs to get out of here somehow. Fighting against her weakness, she assesses her chances. The chamber door is bolted shut from the inside. She'd never be able to lift the massive bolt on her own—not in her present state, anyway.

Eshmun mumbles to himself as he paces erratically beside the bed, his brow furrowed with anxiety. Every so often he leans in over Pius to check on him.

A sudden loud knock at the door makes Eshmun jump nervously before scampering to answer it.

Herodus storms in and approaches the bed, leaving the door ajar. 'Something is wrong, Eshmun. Do something!'

'Herodus, please. The female healer foretold that the recovery will be slow; we must have patience.'

Max keeps her eyes closed and prays they don't notice she's awake.

'I have spoken with the others,' Herodus says, 'and they are anxious to see his progress.'

'What!' Eshmun yells at him. 'You fool! What if the healer has deceived us? What if Pius fails to wake? They will throw us into the lion pit for conspiring with a witch.'

A witch! Max's eyes pop open. She closes them instantly, then sneaks a peek. The expression on Herodus's face tells her that he hadn't thought of that. She wonders who 'the others' are and why these two feel so threatened by them.

'Perhaps,' Herodus sneers, 'if you were as well gifted a healer as you claim to be, we would not find ourselves in this predicament.'

'So the blame falls to me, does it?' Eshmun

retaliates. 'It is not I who has impulsively informed our nobles of Pius's condition and heightened their hope, my friend. I will make sure you face the lions alone.'

'Why, you jackal!' Herodus shouts back at him. 'You will so easily betray me, then?'

Before Max knows what's happening, the men dive at each other, one knocking the other to the floor. Fists fly, but Eshmun's cries of help attract two burly guards who come running in. They yank Herodus off the smaller man and restrain him in the corner of the room.

The door is now wide open, and Max, seeing her chance to escape, makes a run for it. But her getaway is short-lived. Just outside the entrance, she slams into a giant of a guard.

Herodus' expression darkens with fury. 'Enough! This madness will cease immediately. You'—he points to Max—'tell me now, healer, for you have run out of time. Have you succeeded? Will our Ancient Leader wake?'

Max looks to where Pius lies motionless. She can't be sure of anything. But her previous experience gives her the confidence to nod her head.

'You are certain of this?' Eshmun asks anxiously.

Max crosses her fingers behind her back. 'I told you, he just needs to rest.'

Herodus eyes her suspiciously for a moment before sending for a servant. A girl, not that much older than herself, enters the chamber and bows her head to him. He orders her to take Max away. 'And do not let her out of your sight,' he calls to the guard assigned to them, 'not even for a moment, understood?'

Max follows in silence as they make their way through the familiar passageways under the stadium. She's dreading where they're taking her, and resigns herself to being locked away in a mouse infested chamber once again. But when they get there, she's pleasantly surprised to find a neat, modestly furnished room. There's a bed, with actual linen, but more importantly, the room has a bathtub. Max almost squeals with pleasure.

'I will have it filled if you like,' the young girl quietly offers after seeing her reaction.

'Oh, sure. That'll be great, thanks.'

'I am at your service.' The servant busies herself preparing the bath.

'Wait, what's your name?' Max asks her.

The girl lowers her eyes to the ground. 'Aelianna,' she answers shyly. She steps back and bows her head. 'I will return shortly.'

'Thank you, Aelianna, that's very kind of you. My name is Max.'

The girl stops in her departure and looks up timidly, seemingly surprised to be spoken to. 'I will return shortly,' she repeats softly.

Max is stumped by this unexpected courtesy. She senses that Aelianna is a good person, and takes an instant liking to her.

Now alone, Max stands a moment to take in her surroundings. The bed looks soft and inviting—she could easily curl up on it right now and fall asleep again. The room is simple, but above anything, it's clean, bright and airy. A small wooden table and a chair sits on one side, and a small, barred window looks out into the gardens. Max walks up to it and sighs, feeling a sense of calm.

She suddenly remembers Ryker, and her eyes sting with the threat of tears. She chokes back a sob.

Aelianna returns with four guards, who carry huge urns of water ready to empty into the tub. She holds a basket filled with food in one hand and a bundle of clothes in the other. After placing the clothes on the bed, Aelianna lays the table with fruit, nuts, cheeses and dried meats from the basket. But with Ryker fresh on her mind, Max finds that she has no stomach for anything.

'Will you bathe first or sit for your meal?' Aelianna asks gently.

Max knows she needs to eat something to build

up her strength. She decides to wash her hands and face before sitting to eat a little, but she finds that everything tastes like cardboard. She then realises that Aelianna is standing by the closed door, waiting.

'Join me, I'm not that hungry, and there's more than enough for two.'

Aelianna backs away, looking suddenly petrified.

Max jumps, alarmed by her reaction. 'What did I say?'

Aelianna stands at the door nervously shaking her head. 'No, no, I could not possibly do that.'

'What? Why not? Aren't you hungry? You look hungry.'

'Oh, forgive me for staring at the food,' she says in a panic. 'Please, I beg you not to tell your master.'

'My master?' Max almost laughs. 'Aelianna, I think you've mistaken me for someone else. Herodus isn't my master.'

Aelianna frowns, looking confused. 'So you are not the wife of the head gate-keeper?'

Max splutters and almost chokes on the water she has just sipped. 'Wife! Where did you get that idea?'

'A woman does not enter a guard's chamber,' she explains, 'unless she is promised to him. And this is his private chamber.'

Max blinks, momentarily dumbstruck. 'No, you've got it wrong; I'm the healer from the challenges.

They've asked me to help Pius. I'm nothing more than a prisoner here.'

Aelianna frowns, apparently struggling to understand what that means.

'Sit with me. Have something.'

Aelianna shakes her head. 'I cannot be seen sitting while attending to you. I thank you for correcting my misunderstanding, but I will stand in wait until you have eaten. Then I will assist with your bathing and dressing. I have brought clean clothes.'

Assist me with bathing!

'Ah, no offense, but that won't be necessary.' Max laughs. 'Look, I understand that you can't sit with me, but please, I insist that you eat something.' She hands her some food.

Aelianna glances around before taking the food. 'Thank you; you are most gracious.'

Max relaxes a little, happy to be sharing her meal. 'Tell me, do you live here, I mean within the fortress?'

Aelianna shakes her head. 'My home is in the forest, but I have been fortunate to secure a position tending to the guards' chambers.'

'Do you like it here?' Max is curious to know more about these people and their lives. She looks at Aelianna and sees an intelligent, softly spoken young lady, far from the savage she was led to believe the forest people to be. In fact, after meeting Medwin and his friends, Max is questioning everything the guards ever told them.

Aelianna shrugs. 'I work hard, and they provide me, as payment, milk and bread for my services. This helps me feed my family. For that, I am most grateful.'

'Tell me about your family, Aelianna.'

She smiles as she thinks of them. 'Apart from my mother and father who are both unwell, I have three very hungry mouths to feed.'

Max is shocked to hear that this tiny waif of a girl has three children. 'Wow, how old are you?'

'I am not yet nineteen.'

Max can understand now why she was looking at the food with such hunger. She didn't mention a father to the children, so Max wonders whether she's having to raise the children on her own. 'Aelianna, can you take some of this food to the children without the guards knowing?'

Aelianna's eyes widen in alarm. 'Oh, no. I cannot take anything more than what is given to me. I am allowed one loaf of bread and a jug of milk.'

'Then have some more. I'll bathe while you eat. There's no need for you to fuss over me, I can do it myself.'

Aelianna hesitantly approaches the table, clearly too tempted to refuse.

Max hurries to strip, then jumps into the tub.

After dunking her head, she scrubs the dirt from her hair with the soap Aelianna brought, then does the same to her skin until it's clean and pink. She even buffs her nails to remove the built-up grime. It's been far too long since she's had the luxury of soap, and she soon feels half human again.

A sound at the door has Aelianna instantly at Max's side being, once again, attentive. Herodus bursts into the room, looking murderous.

Max lets out a shriek. 'What the hell do you think you're doing? I'm having a bath!'

'I can see that, woman. I do have eyes,' he yells at her.

Max can't believe it; he's still standing there, watching. 'Can I please have some privacy, then?'

'Privacy? May I remind you that this is my chamber. But enough! You have taken more time to bathe than necessary. You have work to do, and Eshmun is waiting.' Herodus storms out of the room, slamming the door behind him.

Aelianna looks like she's on the verge of crying.

And for reasons unbeknown to her, Max starts to giggle. Aelianna tries to shush her, but this makes her giggle more. Soon the two burst into uncontrollable laughter with one shushing the other.

But Herodus is waiting. Max quickly snaps back to reality and tries to compose herself. 'Okay, we'd better hurry up before he comes back. Pack away the food stuff, Aelianna, while I get dressed.'

Max struggles with the toga Aelianna brought for her to wear. But with the girl's help, she gets dressed and ready in no time. Max slips on a pair of Roman sandals just as Herodus enters the room again.

Geez ... if looks could kill ...

Without a word, Max follows him to the Ancient Leader's chamber, and on entering, she sees that they're not alone. The four nobles surround Pius. They turn to her, and she senses they're not happy.

On Herodus' nod, Max hesitantly moves towards the bed. The nobles hover protectively around the Ancient Ruler. She slowly reaches out to place her hand on his forehead. The nobles mutter their disapproval, but Eshmun reassures them and then motions to Max to go on.

She continues. Max feels no tingling in her finger tips or heat radiating from her core. She moves her hand onto his chest, over his heart. Again, she senses no healing energy. She assesses for injured organs and broken bones ... nothing. All signs point to him being in a state of restful sleep.

But before she has a chance to tell them this, the nobles turn on her. 'You claim to have healed him,' one of them cries out. 'I think not! You have deceived us. We see no sign of life here.'

'What kind of dark magic is this?' accuses another. 'His appearance is as he was before the tragedy, but with all our efforts he cannot be stirred.'

'You have killed many,' the third one says. 'You deserve nothing less than being thrown to the lions for your role in this.'

Terrified, Max turns to Herodus and Eshmun for help, but they cower away from the attack. She has to face the wrath of four furious Ancients alone.

'Pius is dead!'

'Your hands are stained with his blood. You must pay for what you have done.'

'Finish her now!'

Max tries to back away but finds herself up against the bed, trapped. Her heart thumps out of control. She looks around, desperate to find a way to escape, but there's nothing that can save her now.

She needs to fight somehow. Her inner voice tells her she can't give up. She has to convince them they're wrong. Through her tears she cries out, 'But he's alive; I promise you. He's just in a deep sleep.'

'You lie!'

'No! Please let me show you,' she begs. But they close in on her. There's no hope now; she's done for. She falls to her knees, covers her face in her hands and begins to sob.

'End her life now!'

'Herodus, hand me your dagger. I will slit her throat and take pleasure in watching her choke on her last breath!'

Dear God, help me!

Max trembles uncontrollably. Any second now and she'll be finished. She thinks of her father, and tears stream down her face as, too late, she realises the love she has for him, and the regret that he'll never know it. She thinks of her Annie, and knows that Annie's heart will break into a million pieces because of her. She thinks of her friends, her Jack. She didn't get a chance to tell him …

'Wait. Look!' a startled voice suddenly cries out.

Max's head jerks up. The point of the dagger hovers mere centimetres above her, but the figure lying on the bed has diverted her executioner's attention.

'Pius lives!' says the ancient healer, Eshmun, who stands by the bedside.

The dagger forgotten, the Ancients rush to assess the miracle before them.

Herodus calls for Aelianna to take Max away. She grabs Max's hand and drags her from the scene. Max is in shock. Her brain has shut down. She's unable to stop shaking and Aelianna struggles to lead her back to the safety of the chamber.

'Hush, hush, you are safe now.' Aelianna holds her in a secure embrace. 'What a horror you have just escaped.'

'I need to get out of here,' Max whispers. A thick fog weighs down her thoughts, and her mind is numb, but she knows she needs to run.

'No, he will be returning. You cannot leave.'

Max tries to shake her thoughts in order. Who can she trust? She thinks of Jack, and suddenly a plan starts to evolve. She looks up at Aelianna. Can she put her faith in this person? What choice does she have? 'Please Aelianna, you need to do something for me.'

'Of course, consider me your friend.'

Max looks into the depths of Aelianna's eyes and knows she means it. 'Believe me, I won't ask you to do anything that will hurt you or your family. All I need for you to do is get a message to my friend. He can help. You mentioned that you live in the forest; do you know Medwin?'

'Yes, I know him well.'

'Go to him and tell him everything you know. Tell him Ryker is dead and I need help. He'll know what to do.'

'Ryker,' she repeats to herself. 'I will go tonight.'

Max squeezes Aelianna's hands. 'Thank you.'

At that moment, Herodus bursts into the chamber. He looks down at their clasped hands and stops. Anger sweeps over his expression. 'Aelianna, go prepare the chamber adjacent to this. I may have a need for it,' he commands.

Aelianna bows respectfully and leaves the room.

'The nobles have asked for you. Come,' he barks out before marching out the door.

Max has trouble keeping up with him as he storms through the passageways. When he stops abruptly, she slams into him from behind.

'Do nothing to anger them, for I will snap you in half if you do,' he threatens. 'Keep your head down, and do not utter a single word. Do you understand?'

Max flinches as though he struck her, but acknowledges her understanding with a nod.

When they enter, Herodus genuflects respectfully, then steps aside for Max. With her eyes lowered to the floor and head bowed, she stands silently, waiting for instruction.

'Come forward, child,' a weak voice calls from the bed. Max looks to Herodus for direction. He motions her to go forward.

She can see the four nobles positioned on either side of Pius, but she keeps her gaze down, avoiding any eye contact.

'You have a special gift,' the Ancient Leader tells her softly. 'Far more advanced than anything we have ever seen.' He pauses to catch his breath. 'Eshmun has told me the extent of my injuries and the strength

94

of your healing.' He pauses again and takes a sip of water. 'We have discussed at length what we should do with you,' he continues, 'and for now, we have decided that you will remain to assist Eshmun in his role as healer. Go now, for I need to rest.' His eyes close, and he's asleep in moments.

Herodus motions for Max to step back. He genuflects again before leaving. Max bows low and follows.

Herodus doesn't say a word until he reaches the chamber next to his own, and then he turns on her in an aggressive manner. 'This is your chamber. You will remain here until either Eshmun or myself come for you.' His unexpected hostility frightens her. 'It is not safe for an unattached woman to venture out of her chamber unescorted. Do you understand?'

She can't understand his anger. She did everything he asked her to do, and she didn't upset the nobles. So why is he so livid?

'You have much work to do, and my task is to keep you alive until your work is done. For your safety it has been declared by the lords that we must wed. No one will dare touch you while you are betrothed to me.'

Betrothed!

Suddenly Max feels as if she's been sucked into a vortex. Sound becomes distant and muffled. Her vision turns hazy, and everything appears to move in slow motion. She looks at Herodus; his mouth moves but no recognisable words come out. Numb with shock, the only thing Max can wrap her head around is the desperate need to get away from him, to hide from the world for a moment while her brain tries to comprehend everything that's just happened.

She nods her head vacantly and slowly backs into the room. Her head feels as if it's about to explode from the pounding in her ears. With weakened limbs, she gropes for something, anything, to support her. Her vision starts to close in. She turns, and seeing nothing in front of her but the bed, she stumbles towards it and collapses in a blissful state of unconsciousness.

13

ℒove!

Jack wakes to a commotion outside his hospital room. He sits up and tries to hear what's happening on the other side of his closed door. The armchair next to his bed is empty, and from what Jack can gather, most of the shouting out there is coming from his father.

'No, you cannot see him! Who do you think you are barging in here at five in the morning demanding anything? If you don't back down right now, mister, I'm going to call security.'

A confident, determined voice with a heavy accent, answers back. 'Do you realise who you're dealing with here? I'm Vice Admiral Engelbrecht. I'm

Ryker's father, and I demand to speak to your son, now. I have just flown from Johannesburg and am anxious to hear what has happened to my boy.'

'Denvon, please,' pleads a softly spoken female voice, 'the poor man is only doing what's best for his son. Be reasonable. Let us sit and talk amicably.'

A somewhat restrained growl comes from the vice admiral before Jack hears him stomp down the corridor and slam a door behind him. The windows shake in his wake.

Jack moves closer and listens as Ryker's mother, Jack guesses, apologises. 'Please forgive him. As you can imagine, we're desperately concerned about our son. We haven't seen or heard from him for over four years. We thought he was dead, so you can guess at our heartache. We need to find out all that we can.'

Before his father has time to answer, Jack steps out of his room. A frail, dishevelled woman stands by Jack's father, mopping at her bloodshot, swollen eyes. She clearly hasn't slept properly in a while.

Jack turns at the sound of a door being flung open at the end of the corridor and heavy footsteps marching towards them. What he sees has him almost turn tail and duck for cover.

'Denvon, let's not do anything rash.' Ryker's mother steps forward to slow his approach.

Oh, crap! This is the man Dad was arguing with?

Ryker's father storms towards them with an entourage of military personnel behind him, each one looking just as determined as their commander. Jack stares, gobsmacked; the man must be over two metres tall and is built like a prize bull. He's a lot like Ryker, but an older version of him and almost twice the size.

Jack's father steps forward and stands with his arms crossed between Jack and the vice admiral.

The disturbance attracts the attention of one of the nurses on duty. 'Now wait just a minute.' Her gaze flashes from one to the other, sizing up the situation, then she hits the red emergency button on the wall and yells, 'Security!'

Jack steps forward to try to calm the situation, but security personnel run in from every direction, and on the vice admiral's command, his men step forward to block their approach. The fathers deliver a cross-fire of threats, each one louder than the other, and the ruckus wakes the other patients from their beds. Banji, Edra and Ulan appear in their doorway and stare in disbelief as the drama unfolds before them.

Jack lets out an ear-piercing whistle which demands everyone's immediate attention. 'Enough of this crap!' he yells. 'Let's all just take a minute and settle down, here.' He turns to security. 'Look, there's no problem here, we just need to talk. Is there somewhere we can do that?'

'You're right, son,' Jack's father says. 'Clearly no one's going to get any peace until they've heard what you kids have to say.' He turns to the vice admiral. 'We're good, right?'

Ryker's dad gestures for his men to fall back.

After assessing the situation and deciding there wasn't going to be any further problems, security take them to a conference room down the corridor.

As they sit to begin their discussion, another two men burst into the room. 'We weren't expecting you so soon,' says the more senior man, hastily adjusting his neck tie as if he'd only just thrown it on. Jack recognises him from the recent news coverage as being the person in charge of the investigation. Captain Logan from the rescue follows close behind.

The first man steps forward and takes charge of the situation. He looks directly at Ryker's father before he begins. 'Vice Admiral Engelbrecht, Mrs Engelbrecht, welcome. We have spoken over the phone. Gerard Thompson, Deputy Director General of Security, ASIO, at your service.' He leans over to shake hands. 'And this is the officer in charge of Task Force Gateway, Captain Dean Logan.'

After saluting the vice-admiral, the captain leans forward and offers his hand. 'It's a pleasure to meet you, sir.'

The deputy director general turns to Jack's dad and extends his hand. 'Daniel, it's good to see you; how's Trish?'

Jack doesn't recognise the man in the suit apart from the media coverage, but clearly he knows his parents.

'Happier to have Jack home, thanks Gerry. Now what's going on? I didn't think their flight was due until noon. The other parents aren't here yet.'

'Professor Rutherford insisted we arrive ASAP in order to start the wheels in motion,' the vice admiral tells them. 'He sent us his private jet.'

Jack is momentarily stumped. *Professor Rutherford? Why does that name sound so familiar?*

But before he can think on it, the door swings open and another man races into the room. He's somewhat younger than Gerard Thompson, more his father's age. Something about him makes Jack sit up and take notice. His eyes are sunken and bloodshot, and his clothes hang from his bony frame as though he's wearing a suit two sizes too big for his body. His face sports a five o'clock shadow at only five in the morning.

Gerard Thompson greets him and shakes his hand. 'Glad you could make it, Edward.'

'Professor Rutherford.' Ryker's father stands

and offers his hand, too. 'I'm Vice Admiral Denvon Engelbrecht, and this is my wife, Isebel.'

'I appreciate you all coming so promptly,' says the professor. He turns to shake Jack's father's hand. 'Daniel, good to see you again. Now, we have much to discuss and organise. Gerard please, don't let me interrupt. The sooner we begin, the sooner I can get my daughter back.'

Suddenly, the only sound Jack can hear is the pounding of his heart. Everything else is white noise. His field of vision starts to constrict to the point where all he can see is the man standing before him—Max's father.

'Son, are you okay?'

It takes Jack more than a moment to compose himself. He shakily turns to his father and gives him a forced smile.

'Okay,' Gerard Thompson begins, 'now, I know you're all anxious to get on with the matter at hand, so I'll turn it over to the kids and get them to describe what we're facing here. Jack, can we begin with you?'

This catches Jack off guard. He's still reeling from the shock of seeing Max's father for the first time. This is the man who's alienated his daughter, the man who's buried his own life with his work, the man responsible for her hang-ups. And then with sudden clarity, Jack sees that she's been wrong—so wrong.

Before him stands a man that hasn't eaten or slept in weeks, a man who's died a thousand deaths since his daughter went missing, a man who loves her with every fibre of his being.

Daniel Braden places a fatherly hand on his son's shoulder, concern etched in the lines of his face. There are so many lines now. *When did he get so old?*

Jack looks around the room and sees the pain in the eyes of everyone scarred by the Ancient Realm. He looks at Ryker's mother, a shadow of a once beautiful woman—her heart bruised and fragile, her eyes begging him to help find her only child. Jack looks at Ryker's father, desperate to bring his boy home and keep him forever out of harm's way. He looks at Edra, broken but desperate to heal with the love of her family. He sees Banji and Ulan, closer than any other twins could ever be, sharing identical scars.

Jack finally looks back into the eyes of his father, and he sees a man that had lost a son, a son that left as a boy and returned a man. Those eyes tell of his pride, his confidence and his never-ending love and support.

Jack draws in a deep breath. He's ready.

He starts from the beginning and doesn't stop until he relays every detail of how they escaped.

'But you think she'll be all right, don't you?' Max's father asks, desperation written in every line of his face. 'There's a good chance she's safe with Ryker, right?'

'Better than good,' Banji interrupts. 'Sir, I've known Ryker most of my life, and I'm sure Max will be okay.'

'And I will second that.' The vice admiral stands and begins to pace with authority. 'My son has been well trained in survival manoeuvres. Before his disappearance, he had spent six years as a cadet. I have every confidence that they have managed to keep out of harm.'

'There's one thing I don't quite get,' Deputy Thompson interrupts. 'Let me try to understand this. You and your group, Jack, had to compete against Ryker and his group in the challenges, correct?'

'That's right.'

'Then how is it that you helped each other escape?'

'Well, that's something that might need a bit of explaining,' Jack begins uneasily. He's hoping he can say this without making Ryker look like the jerk that he was. 'It must seem weird, but at first we were sworn enemies—we had to be. Ryker's team were desperate to win, just like we were. It was cut throat; we literally had to fight to survive. Both sides copped their fair share of injuries in these challenges. If it wasn't for Max, the end result could've been very different.'

Jack can see that Deputy Thompson is waiting for

more, so he turns to Edra for some support because what he has to say next may not go down too well.

'You have to understand,' Edra says, 'that after four years, Ryker had changed—we all had. But with him, it was different. He'd reached a point where he kind of snapped. He wasn't himself anymore.'

Ryker's mother reaches out for her husband's hand for support.

Edra reluctantly continues. 'After one of the challenges which left our team severely beaten up, Ryker could see that our chance for ever escaping was slipping away, so he … well, he became desperate … he kidnapped Max.'

'What?' Max's father jumps up, marches straight up to the vice admiral and pokes him in the chest. 'Your son abducted my daughter, and now she's there alone with him! So help me, God, if he lays one finger on her, there'll be hell to pay. Call the police; I'm pressing charges.'

'How dare you!' the bigger man threatens.

It's an uneven match by a long shot. Jack can see it turning ugly, real fast. 'Stop!' he yells at them. 'Let Edra finish.'

The room goes suddenly silent. Both men step back and make an effort to compose themselves.

Edra tries again: 'Ryker did what he did because we were so beaten up, we couldn't compete anymore.

He did it so Max could fix our injuries. You're right, at the time it was the wrong thing to do, but in the end, it was the catalyst that helped us escape.' She looks from Ryker's father to Max's. 'It was Max who helped him see that what he was doing was wrong. He nearly died after one of the challenges, and Max saved him and turned his life around. He loves her and would protect her with his life.'

LOVE!

Jack suddenly can't breathe.

'Love! That's my little girl you're talking about,' the professor says. 'What the hell is going on here?'

'Please, everyone. Let's just settle down for a minute.' Deputy Thompson steps forward to calm the situation. 'We need to work together on this. Remember, your children's lives are at stake here.'

It takes a moment for everyone to calm down and take their seats.

'I can see now how an alliance was formed,' Deputy Thompson continues. 'You guys have shown a maturity beyond your years. Maybe we can all take a leaf out of your book. But there's still a lot to digest here. The whole situation, quite frankly, is nothing like we've ever come across. There are things that we need to discuss before we even consider trying to penetrate this Ancient Realm to rescue your children.'

He looks at Ryker's father. 'Vice Admiral

Engelbrecht has, of course, come with a group of his top men to assist with the assembling of the special task force we're in the process of putting together—one specific to this unique situation. Captain Logan will have the opportunity to fill you in on his progress there. Unfortunately, we don't have the luxury of time on our side. We need to act swiftly and as efficiently as possible. We need to study the situation thoroughly and be well informed before we attack. This is where you kids are key.' He turns to Jack. 'We need to get as much information from you as we can. Any detail that you can give us may prove to be vital. Ruby, Kenny and Peanut will be joining us shortly so we can have their input as well.'

'Hang on a sec,' Jack jumps up, suddenly angered. 'You're talking as if you're going back in there without us.'

'Jack, you can't be serious!' His father gets up and rests his hand firmly on his son's shoulder. 'Surely you're not thinking to join them?'

'Dad,' Jack takes his father's hand and looks him square in the eye, 'there's no questioning my call on this one. My team have already decided; we're committed to finishing this thing together. I can't talk for Edra and the twins, but Peanut, Ruby, Kenny and I are going.'

'Well, son, that's admirable,' Ryker's father says.

'We can see that you want to help, and rest assured that you will be, by providing us with as much information as possible. We won't be taking any of you with us. We can't risk anyone getting hurt.'

Jack shakes his head. 'Sorry, sir, this is not negotiable.'

'Jack, you're not thinking straight!' his father says. 'Think about it. You're injured. How are you supposed to help in your condition?'

'Dad, you guys need us,' Jack argues. 'And as for my injury, when I pass through to the other side, it won't be a problem anymore. Don't you get it?'

Jack watches as his father struggles with this decision.

'Max saved my life. I won't abandon her, okay?'

They're wasting precious time. Jack needs to take control. He turns to face Deputy Thompson. 'I've already told you that once we pass into this ancient realm, our superpowers get ignited. Kenny's our go-to man for information, and as you know, I develop superhuman endurance. But what I haven't told you yet is that Ruby can whip up an impenetrable shield, and Peanut has the ability to become invisible. So let's start talking strategy.'

14

Another World

Max

Max slowly stirs to consciousness. Her eyelids feel heavy and her head throbs. She raises her fingertips to her temples and feels soothing heat flow from them as she starts to heal. It takes her no time to remember all that happened last night. She curls herself into a ball and starts to cry. She just wants to die. *Betrothed? They should've just killed me!*

But what does that mean, exactly? Is it, as Herodus said, only to keep away the other guards while they use her to fix the wounded, or will it give him rights to touch her? Her stomach turns. She snatches a bowl from the side of her bed in time to throw up in it. Herodus' rage at the nobles' command suggests that he wasn't too thrilled with the idea, either. She feels a little better knowing this.

A sound at the door puts Max on the defensive. She runs to the other side of the room as her husband-to-be barges in.

'You are required to assist Eshmun. I will return shortly to take you to him,' he says, then leaves the room as abruptly as he came.

In his wake, the timid servant girl, Aelianna, enters with a platter of food and rests it on the table. She keeps her eyes diverted and only on Herodus exiting does she chance a brief glance at Max. That fleeting look manages to convey a message, and Max realises that she wasn't able to get her message to Medwin last night.

But that doesn't mean that I should give up, right? Help's on its way. For now, just keep your nose clean and do what they tell you to do.

Knowing that they'll soon come for her, she makes an effort to eat something. But it's all dry and tasteless to her, and she struggles to keep any of it down—she may as well be eating sawdust.

Her thoughts are consumed with what will happen now. How many people were injured in the devastation, and will she be able to cope? What if she can't? But she already knows the answer to that one …

Herodus' sudden appearance at the door startles her. She jumps up, and without a word, rushes to follow him. He takes her through the tangle of corridors. The numerous dark, cold passageways become a meshwork of confusion. Even if she'd wanted to escape at that moment, she'd never be able to find her way out.

The sound of lively activity comes from up ahead. Low chatter mixed with occasional shouting become more distinct as they make their way closer to the commotion. The tunnel leads them to a brightly lit exit where the activity is at its highest. Incredibly, she can hear what sounds to be a hive of daily activity, a marketplace. And then suddenly she's amongst it, surrounded by hundreds of people scurrying about their daily activities.

All her senses come alive, but the brilliance of the sudden change in lighting momentarily blinds her. She shields her eyes from the glare and struggles to keep them open to see what's happening around her and where she's being taken.

'Keep up!' Herodus growls at her.

Her eyes stream with tears as she tries to keep him in her sights. She dodges a few tearaway kids and some carefree farm animals. Unfamiliar aromas invade her senses—unusual spices and cooking smells— all mixed with something she recognises instantly when she steps in a warm, offensive-smelling, brown mound left behind by the beast casually ambling some way in front of her.

'Aah! Gross!'

But she doesn't have time for that. Her gaze darts around, trying to take in all she's seeing. People go about with their purchases. Oxen draw carts, and armed guards ride on horses. The place is huge. And just beyond the shaded stalls of the vendors and the crowds, rise double-storeyed buildings, shoulder to shoulder, encasing the market place. The buildings go as far as her eye can see, with washed clothing dangling from the balconies, saluting gently in the wind.

So this is where the spectators come from.

Max glimpses Herodus ahead of her looking like he's about to dart into a building. For a split second, she considers losing herself in the crowd but the moment she contemplates the idea, his steely eyes lock onto hers. The threat delivered with that gaze has her running to his side in an instant.

She follows him through the entrance which eventually leads to a large courtyard where scores of injured people are lying and moaning in pain. Leaning over one of them is a figure draped in a black cloak, Eshmun.

'At last!' He gets to his feet as soon as he sees

them. 'Quickly, get her to work. Two more have died this morning.'

Herodus turns on Max. 'You have created this mayhem, now fix it!'

Max glances around in horror at what looks like a bloodied battle field and wonders where on earth she should start. A violent shove from Herodus makes it clear that here is as good a place to start as any.

She stares down at the man Eshmun has been attending to. He's lost a lot of blood, and her senses tell her that he doesn't have long to live. She jumps into action—if he dies on her, there's no knowing what they'll do to punish her.

She searches for a pulse but can't find one, then listens for a breath and finds barely a hint of life. She needs to perform CPR. She tilts his head up and blows two breaths into his lungs, then prepares to push down on his chest. With the first compression, she feels and hears his ribs snap under the weight. She jerks back, alarmed. Would she do more harm than good by continuing? She needs to fix his ribs first. The heat in her belly fires up instantly and projects to her fingertips in seconds. She hears the bones clicking into place, but she doesn't stop until she feels confident that they've strengthened enough to cope with the continuation of the compressions. When she starts again, she realises that she isn't strong enough for the ongoing effort it'll take to press down hard enough. She needs Eshmun to help.

'Here,' she tells him, 'repeat what I've just done as soon as I've given him some air.'

But the ancient healer withdraws in horror.

'If you don't do this, he'll die!'

Eshmun frowns but hesitantly places his hands on the patient's chest, then mimics Max's earlier actions. Very soon they have a rhythm going, and once Max senses a strong and steady heartbeat, she continues to heal the rest of him.

Eshmun brings her some water before she moves onto the next person.

But even with Eshmun assisting, Max quickly becomes exhausted. 'I need to rest,' she says after the first few patients.

Herodus glares at her. 'You will continue until we say it is time to stop.'

This indicates what will be expected of her during the course of her captivity.

To keep Herodus off her back, Max pushes through her own pain and suffering. Victim after victim are brought to her to heal, and when she's reached a point beyond being of any use to them, he lets her sleep—but only long enough for a brief recharge, and then he wakes her to continue.

Broken bones, internal bleeding, crushed skulls

… repeat.

At the end of the day, they have to call a guard to carry her limp body back to her chamber. They leave her there to recover for a few hours before the whole scenario starts up again.

The days soon blend into one. Max loses track of time and can no longer tell night from day. She vaguely recalls Aelianna hovering and fretting over her, trying to encourage her to eat something. And she tries to—she knows she needs to get her strength from somewhere. But she doesn't have the power to remain upright most of the time, let alone eat anything. Her only solace comes when, at the end of each day, she feels the bed beneath her tortured body and the silent protective shroud of darkness descends.

15

THE WINDS OF CHANGE

RYKER

Four days have passed without any word on Max. There's no talk of her fate amongst the forest people, no news to reassure Ryker that she's still even alive.

'Why haven't we heard anything?' he growls in frustration to Medwin.

Both men are sitting by the stream, securing into bundles the fish Ryker has caught.

'I grant you; it is most unusual. We know nothing about your friend, nor the consequences of Slade's deceit.'

'I'm going mad here; I need to know that Max is okay.'

'All in good time, my friend.'

'Medwin, you're driving me nuts. What exactly are we waiting for?' Ryker's patience is wearing thin. 'I should've just marched up to them and volunteered myself as Beowulf's replacement like I originally thought to do. I don't know why I let you talk me out of it in the first place.'

'We have already spoken of this being a bad decision, Ryker, and you know it. You are an enemy to The Ancients. You have shown your allegiance to the healer and her friends. The Ancients will imprison you the moment you step up to their doorstep. You need another strategy.'

'I've been racking my brain trying to come up with one. I've got nothing.'

'Patience. The solution has not revealed itself to you because the time has not been favourable. Rest assured that when that hour comes, you will know the direction of your fate. And since you are so anxious to have a resolution, I can now tell you this: I woke this morning with a premonition. Deep within my bones I feel that the winds are about to change.'

Ryker looks sceptically at him from the corner of his eyes.

'Have faith in what I am telling you, my friend.'

Ryker lets out a frustrated breath. 'These winds had better hurry up and change, then!'

They sit in silence, finishing the bundles.

'Medwin, what are we doing here? Why have we caught so many fish today?' Ryker looks at the mound they're working on.

'I intend to visit a friend; the fish are for her. Poor child, she has six mouths to feed and struggles to bring home enough food.'

'What about her husband, why doesn't he provide for them?'

'Oh, Aelianna has no husband. She has an invalid father, a sick mother and three children to support, one being simple minded from birth.'

Ryker hears a soft cry from the woods and jumps up. 'Did you hear that? Someone's calling out to you.'

Medwin stands to listen, and this time he hears it, too. Eyes alive with excitement, he makes his way towards the sound. Ryker begins to follow, but Medwin signals for him to remain. 'Do not concern yourself. I shall be safe and will return shortly.'

Ryker remains standing and anxiously awaits his return.

After a few minutes, Medwin emerges, smiling.

'What do you smile about, old man?' Ryker asks, feeling less guarded but curious.

'You, too, will be smiling at the news brought in

on the winds of change.'

'What news?'

Medwin laughs. 'Ah, my curious friend, you will be surprised to hear how powerful my gift of intuition and foresight truly is.'

'Will you stop talking in riddles and just tell me? Is it news on Max?'

'We were just talking of my friend, Aelianna, were we not?'

'Medwin,' Ryker growls, 'will you cut to the chase?'

'I am not quite clear on your meaning, my friend, but it is not a coincidence that we have only just spoken her name. It was she who called me into the forest. She has come with word directly from your friend.'

'Max!' Ryker is about to burst from the need to know more.

'You must sit quietly and listen without excitement, for the forest has eyes and ears.'

Ryker looks about them, on guard.

'Aelianna has news, but cannot reveal herself as she is being constantly followed by Herodus or one of his henchmen. It has taken her two days to evade them. She has taken a great risk coming to us today.'

Ryker tries to calm down, not wanting to interrupt Medwin.

'It has been arranged that I will meet with her at nightfall in the guise of bringing her family the fish we have caught. This will not appear suspicious since I often take surplus food to her family. You will follow without being seen, under the protection of the night sky.'

'No, Medwin, I can't wait. I need to talk to her, now!'

Medwin puts up his hand to stop him. 'What you want and what will happen are two very different things. As an enemy to the Ancients, anyone seen with you will immediately be tarred the same. I will not allow any harm to come to Aelianna or her family. You have no choice but to be patient.'

Ryker feels torn. His immediate reaction is to go after the woman, but at the same time, he hears what Medwin is saying; the consequences of accosting her now could be disastrous for her.

He takes a moment to calm himself and think things through. 'You're right. Of course, you're right. I'm sorry. Medwin, I hear what you're saying, and I get it—really, I do—but I'm struggling here. Max is important to me, and I made a promise to protect her.'

'You speak of your friend with great affection,' Medwin eyes him with curiosity. 'Could it be that you have formed an attachment?'

Ryker frowns at the question. 'It's hard to explain,' he says honestly. 'Even I don't get it, but somehow I'm a better person when I'm with her. She grounds me.'

'It sounds to me very much like an attachment …' Medwin stops midstream, clearly having foreseen something. 'But alas, it will not eventuate,' he reveals cryptically before casually gathering up his bundles of fish ready to go.

'What do you mean?'

Medwin smiles. 'I will return at nightfall.'

'Medwin!'

But Medwin disappears into the forest, leaving Ryker with his question unanswered.

16

THE BEAST

When the sun begins to set and the night animals stir, Ryker descends from the treehouse anxious to meet Medwin's friend. He prays that she has good news. If he finds out that Max has been harmed in any way, he's going to lose it.

He tries to keep his thoughts positive as he makes his way to the meeting place. Thankfully, cloud cover blankets the night sky, making it easier for him to move about without being seen.

Medwin has been waiting and is ready when he arrives. They head off immediately and soon enter an area unfamiliar to Ryker. The woods thin out, revealing small mud-brick dwellings, clustered together. Through the open windows of each humble, thatched-roof cottage, he glimpses families within sitting at their meal. The ambient glow of the fireplaces shed soft light throughout the homes.

Medwin gestures for him to stay hidden, then approaches a home and knocks quietly at the door.

Ryker watches from a distance as the wooden door creaks ajar and a small figure peeks out. A huge smile lights up the young woman's face when she recognises her visitor. She opens the door wide and steps aside to let him in.

Ryker's breath catches at the sight of her, and he falls back, winded. *Wow!* The effect she has on him—racing heart, sweaty palms—momentarily sideswipes him. He shakes his head to make some sense of this reaction and to clear his befuddled thoughts. He has to remind himself to breathe.

Get a grip! You're here for Max.

He takes a few deep breaths to calm himself and tries to focus on the task at hand. For the millionth time today, he wonders what Medwin's friend has to tell them.

As he's considering this, the door opens again to reveal the same pretty girl, and then their mutual friend leads her directly towards him. Ryker steps back into the darkness. Again, his heart starts to race. He looks anxiously around, suddenly desperate to take off into the woods. But try as he might, he finds that he can't—his feet suddenly feel like lead weights. Before he has the chance to do anything, Medwin arrives and introduces him to the most beautiful, heavenly creature he has ever seen.

Ryker's mouth goes so dry he can't talk—he almost gags trying. And so he meets this ethereal vision before him with stunned silence.

This can't be Aelianna, the person Medwin was talking about, the one with three children. She isn't that much older than Max.

Medwin glares at him, trying to prompt him to ask his questions. '… and Aelianna, allow me to introduce you to Ryker. He is most anxious to hear about his friend.'

Ryker tentatively steps out from the darkness. 'Y-you're Aelianna?'

Her reaction startles him. She sweeps her gaze over him and takes a few steps back.

'Do not have fear, my child,' Medwin assures her. 'You are safe. Despite his intimidating size, Ryker has a good and gentle heart.'

'Ryker?' Her eyes widen, and her mouth opens then closes as if suddenly speechless.

Medwin looks at her with concern, his brow furrowed.

'F-forgive me,' she replies awkwardly. 'It's just

that we thought you were dead—that is to say, Max did.'

'Dead?' This snaps Ryker back to attention.

'It is true, Max believes you to be dead.' She lowers her face and looks away. A flush of pink stains her cheeks.

Ryker immediately misses looking into her beautiful, deep-brown eyes. 'Well, as you can see,' he teases, 'I'm not.'

Her eyes lock onto his again and her face lights up. 'We can be thankful, then, that she has been mistaken.'

Medwin stands mute between them, looking from one to the other, waiting to hear the conversation progress, but the two appear suddenly tongue-tied. 'So what news of the healer?' he prompts.

Aelianna breaks her gaze with Ryker, then blinks a few times and slowly shakes her head before telling them about Max.

Ryker, too, takes a few seconds to regroup. He listens carefully, and as she reveals how poorly they've been treating Max, his blood begins to boil. 'Damn it, I need to get in there! I can't protect her while I'm out here!'

Aelianna's eyes go wide at his tone.

Medwin places a supportive hand on his arm. 'I know of your anxiety, Ryker, but how can you get past the guards? For certain, you will be found out and imprisoned. You'll be more than useless to her then.'

'I won't need to break in, I still think I can convince Herodus that I'd make a good replacement for Beowulf. Surely I'm worth more to them alive than dead.'

'My friend,' Medwin argues, 'if you need to *convince* them to take you, then they will become suspicious of your motives. Remember, you have just spent the last four years trying to escape, and now you are asking them to take you back? Think clearly on it before you act hastily.'

'Then it is simple,' Aelianna's soft voice breaks through Ryker's thoughts. 'Your plan will work only if you let it come about by their hand.'

Ryker frowns. 'I don't understand.'

Medwin claps his hands with excitement. 'But of course!' He chuckles. 'Aelianna, my child, your wisdom matches your beauty. Why had I not considered this myself?'

Though Ryker doesn't understand what caused it, Medwin's sudden enthusiasm makes him feel more hopeful.

'This is what will happen,' Medwin explains. 'Ryker, you will not volunteer yourself to Herodus; instead we will lure him to you.' He pauses to let his ingenious idea take root before continuing, 'We will remind him of your worth. He is not so foolish as to ignore someone with the strength you possess.'

Ryker sees a plan hatching. He smiles at Aelianna, impressed with her way of thinking. 'So what do you suggest we do?' he asks Medwin.

'We know Aelianna is being watched,' Medwin says as he considers this, 'so she can lead his men to you.'

Although Ryker thinks this is a good idea, something doesn't sit well with him. He looks at Aelianna's eager face. He couldn't have her risk so much. 'But it's not safe for Aelianna. I don't want her involved any more than she already is.'

The sparkle in her eyes suddenly disappears.

'Don't get me wrong,' he's quick to tell her. 'I'm truly grateful for what you've already done, but I couldn't ask you to do this. It's far too dangerous.' He can't believe that this gorgeous creature is so eager to help him. His heart swells.

'Max has been good to me,' Aelianna says, 'I cannot withstand seeing her suffer as she does, so it would be nothing for me to help.'

Ryker looks away, embarrassed that he got it so wrong. Of course, she's doing this for Max. He gives himself a mental blasting back to reality. He smiles awkwardly. 'Then Max is a lucky girl to have a friend like you.'

'If I can lead Herodus into the forest, then let me do it. I will not need to be any further involved than that,' she tells him.

He looks into her imploring eyes and is immediately mesmerised once again. He shakes his head, gives himself another mental warning and turns his focus to Medwin, who is all seriousness. This helps ground him.

There's no doubt in his mind that with Aelianna's help, this could work. He takes a moment to consider everything, then makes the decision. 'Okay, we'll do it, but only if we can be certain of your safety, Aelianna.'

Her face lights up with happiness. And just as before, Ryker's heart skips a few beats at the sight of it.

Medwin makes a move to leave, bursting Ryker's bubble of joy. 'My child, you have risked much seeing us tonight,' he says to Aelianna. 'We will leave you now to put together our thoughts. I will return on the morrow with a plot.'

The spell is broken, and Ryker is strangely relieved that their meeting has come to an end. He doesn't know what's gotten into him. He stops to remind himself that, smile or no smile, he's here for Max. He needs to get away—and fast.

'Oh, must you leave so soon?' Aelianna asks, her

face open and eager. 'Why not come in for some refreshments? I have a little wine for such occasions.'

For reasons beyond his comprehension, Ryker turns with excitement, ready to accept. But thankfully, Medwin interrupts before he gets a chance to do so. 'You are most gracious, my child. Thank you all the same, but the hour is late and we will not impose on you or your family any longer. Good night.'

Aelianna's expression drops, her disappointment clear, and she seems reluctant when she says good night and returns to her home. This surprises Ryker.

What the hell is going on here? Get a grip, man. He tries to shake the confusion from his head. 'Medwin, let's get out of here!' he says. And with newfound determination, Ryker forges his way back towards the treehouse. He doesn't stop until they're well away from those warm, dark, tantalising eyes.

That was close!

But exactly what he just escaped, he has no idea. This emotional roller-coaster ride he's on makes his head spin. This girl has him questioning which way is up. As they walk away, he wonders about her and her life. He wants to know more about the father of her children. *Why isn't he around?*

'Ryker, you must keep your wits about you,' Medwin warns. 'There is much for us to consider. Get your head out from the clouds.'

Ryker realises with embarrassment how transparent his thoughts have been. 'Tell me something, why is Aelianna bringing up the children on her own? Where's their father?'

Medwin stops and scratches his head, looking very confused. 'But I have already told you, he is an invalid. Aelianna cares for him.'

Ryker also comes to a halt, just as confused. 'I know, but what about the children's father? Where is he?'

Medwin looks at Ryker as if he'd just grown a second head.

'What did I say?'

Ryker watches as realisation dawns on the smaller man. 'Oh, I comprehend your misunderstanding now. You are believing that the children are her own, are you not?'

'Yeah, you said that she supports her mother, father and her three children,' he reminds him.

Medwin chuckles. 'Aelianna has no husband, nor has she any children of her own. The three that I have mentioned are her two brothers and her sister.'

'Oh!' This new understanding leaves Ryker momentarily speechless and then confused by the unexpected emotions of relief and excitement he feels.

'Aelianna is the eldest of four children,' Medwin

explains. 'Her brother Felix, the simple minded one, is next in age, then there is Sigrun, and last is Afon. Their mother became ill after the birth of Afon, so Aelianna has brought up the child as her own. Their father, Molan was injured some time ago. Remember I told you of him. He was our village's chief hunter. He fell down a ravine and has been bed-ridden ever since.'

Ryker remains silent as he takes that all in. He can't begin to imagine how tough life has been for someone so young.

Medwin then smiles mischievously. 'And you will get to know each of them soon enough.'

'What do you mean?'

'Oh, all will be revealed in good time, my young friend.'

It's clear by Medwin's look and cryptic message that he's seen something in Ryker's future. But tempting as it is to find out more, Ryker ignores his friend's teasing.

'Come on, let's get out of here.'

Ryker is thankful that the journey back to the treehouse is a silent one. He doesn't allow himself to reflect on Medwin's words. First and foremost, they need to plan a deception, after that they need to save a friend. And that's all he allows himself to think about … for now.

17

DARE TO DREAM

The plan is set. Aelianna's been informed of the plot and given instructions. She's not to tell a soul about what they're about to do, not even Max.

Aelianna goes through the strategy again and again as she goes about her daily chores. She needs to be prepared for anything, so she goes over every possible complication that she may encounter. They'll only get one chance to get this right, and she doesn't want to be the reason for its failure.

As she busies herself replacing the bedsheets and freshening the guard's chambers, she visualises what might eventuate later today. On her way home, she is to pass by the stream and lure her follower to Ryker, who will be busy exhibiting his strength in the best possible light.

Her heart races at the thought of seeing him again. She fans her flushed face and tries to steady her accelerated breathing. 'Enough!' she quietly tells herself. But when she struggles to wipe the silly grin off of her face, she realises that she's fighting a losing battle.

The first moment she laid eyes on him, she lost control of her senses. He consumes her every waking thought. His magnetic smile instantly melts her into a puddle, and the power of his life force makes her want to curl up safely in his massive arms and stay there forever. She hardly knows who she is anymore.

Her head spins from all these unfamiliar feelings and confusing thoughts. The rush she gets when she thinks of him—the pain in her chest; the butterflies in her stomach—terrifies her, but she wants it … she wants it all.

What is happening to me!

Her sensible-self keeps telling her to stay away from the handsome stranger, but the young woman inside her cries out to follow her heart. She stops abruptly and compels herself to think about what she's about to do. Is she making a mistake? But she knows the answer to that. 'No, Max needs me.'

Aelianna is close to tears when she thinks of how

they've been mistreating her new friend. Day after day she watches her collapse onto her bed, starved and exhausted, only to be woken in the early hours of the morning to be put back to work. 'Oh, poor Max!'

The sound of something scurrying by the door has Aelianna turn in a panic. Terrified that she may have been heard, she runs to investigate. She sees the culprit darting down the passageway and quickly make its escape through a crack in the wall. Thankfully it's just a rat. She takes in a shaky breath to settle her frayed nerves and succeeds in making it through the rest of the day without uttering another unguarded word.

When she meets Max later that evening, she's alarmed to see how much she has deteriorated since she last saw her. But she refrains from reacting. She goes about doing her duties and keeping the conversation distant. Thankfully, Max doesn't have the strength to question her about her altered behaviour.

Aelianna helps her bathe, then dress. She tries to encourage her to eat something but has trouble keeping her awake long enough to finish one mouthful.

'It is time for you to leave,' Herodus says loudly as he enters the chamber.

His sudden appearance makes Aelianna jump. 'Of course,' she says respectfully as she prepares to leave the room.

'What makes you startle so?' he asks suspiciously.

She lowers her gaze and remains silent.

Herodus studies her for a moment longer before dismissing her.

She quickly makes her way to the kitchen to receive her pay, then hurries past the guards on the drawbridge and makes a beeline to the stream.

The sun is starting to set. The window of opportunity is closing fast. It'll be dark soon, possibly too dark for Herodus to witness Ryker at work. She quickens the pace, her heart pounding in her chest like a wild, caged animal trying to escape. She can't afford to make a mistake now. Her friend's life depends upon it.

She nears the stream, her anticipation escalating. She should be able to hear Ryker by now, but her breathing is so laboured that it's difficult to hear anything over it. She slows down and closes her eyes. Her breathing calms, and finally she hears him.

The rhythmical sound of an axe hacking at a tree brings unexpected tears of joy to her eyes. She can't understand her reaction and shakes off her nonsense. It's time to put on a performance.

Reining in her excitement, she creeps closer and squats behind a bush to spy on him. She needs to act surprised and then impressed at what she sees, so as to pique her follower's interest.

Ryker has been hard at it, it would seem. He's already half constructed and assembled a treehouse, and his shirt clings to his sweaty body from the effort he's making. You would need to be half blind not to be impressed by what she's seeing. There's no need for any pretence here. Ryker, indeed, is an impressive specimen of a man.

Aelianna tries to quell her elation and listens to hear if she's his only audience. A distant crack from a twig under foot confirms, almost certainly, that she's not. She relaxes a little, sits back and allows herself to enjoy the show, which proves to be quite the challenge. What she's witnessing has her struggling to keep a goofy smile from giving herself away. She enjoys watching Ryker so much that she needs to bite the inside of her cheek to stop the grin appearing.

She watches Ryker fell the enormous tree he's hacking at, pick it up—with minimal exertion—and split the trunk into thin strips. He then straps the split wood to his back and effortlessly hauls the heavy load up the trunk of the treehouse where, one by one, he ties the wood to form the floor. What he's doing genuinely mesmerises Aelianna because she's never seen it done before.

Ryker's performance exceeds even her own expectations. Just by looking at him, it's clear that the man is strong, but witnessing him in action is another thing entirely. Although she'd love to remain and watch the whole performance, she knows that she needs to make her way home. It's crucial to the plan that she's seen to have no association with him.

So Aelianna carefully and quietly continues on her way. She says a silent prayer to all the Gods of Mercy, Empathy and Charity that everything has gone to plan.

And once inside her little home she allows herself to smile and enjoy the giddy feeling that that smile gives her as she thinks of her co-conspirator. She closes her eyes, replays the images she has of him, and dares to dream that one day he might feel the same about her.

18

I Hope You Know What You're Doing

Ryker has been working up a sweat for a few hours now. The pace he's been keeping is gruelling, but he won't let up because his demonstration needs to be convincing—*for Max's sake*, he constantly reminds himself.

His senses are on high alert anticipating Herodus' approach, but there's been no sign of him, and Ryker's starting to worry. *Man, if he doesn't show up soon, I'll be forced to make another stupid treehouse!*

He allows his thoughts to go to Aelianna, and suddenly his blood turns to ice. *What if something's happened to her!*

Before he has time to panic, several guards charge at him from the woods, knock him to the ground and throw a large net over him. Although prepared for the assault, Ryker is momentarily stunned. But he recovers quickly and begins to claw at the net, determined to put on a good show. He puts up a decent fight, letting out an enormous roar as he protests against the restraints, but surprisingly, he very quickly finds himself well and truly trapped.

Herodus appears before him. 'Ryker, it is good to see you again, old friend. But it would appear that you are in a bit of a tangle.' He laughs.

'Friend? If you treat your friends like this, then I'd hate to see how you treat your enemies.'

'Oh, how I have missed our stimulating banter.'

Ryker lets out a growl of exasperation.

'I see that your friends have managed to escape but left you behind. You may be interested to hear that your healer has been captured and is being punished as is her due.'

Ryker's blood starts to boil, but he tries not to react. He knows Herodus is baiting him. In order to gain his trust, he needs to convince Herodus that he has no alliance with Max. 'You're mistaken; she's not my healer. And what do I care about her, anyway? You can do what you like with her.'

'Correct me if I am wrong,' Herodus eyes him suspiciously, 'but did you not go to great lengths to save her at the gateway?'

Ryker groans loudly. 'It was stupid, impulsive and the biggest mistake I've ever made. That *healer* might have saved my life, but she's cost me my freedom!' he yells. 'So, like I said, do what you like with her. She means nothing to me.'

Herodus studies Ryker for a long while before answering. 'Interesting. I'm in two minds whether to believe you. But let us not argue for I have a more pressing issue to discuss.'

'Is that right? And what would that be?'

But the answer to that falls on deafened ears. A sudden blow to his head knocks Ryker out.

'The issue, dear friend,' Herodus chuckles, 'is that perhaps it is time for us to revisit the arena, for old-times' sake. What say you? Nothing? Hmm … well, then it is agreed upon.'

Medwin, hidden out of sight, witnesses the attack. He cringes at the brutality but can do nothing to help his friend. Yes, the plan has worked, but it's difficult to watch just the same. He looks on as the guards hog-tie Ryker's wrists and feet. They then tighten the net around him and drag his limp body through the forest and out of sight.

'I do hope you know what you are doing, my friend.'

19

The Cheshire Cat

Jack

It's killing him. Everything's moving at a snail's pace. Jack can't believe all the red tape involved in getting anything done. There's always someone who needs to be answered to, who then needs to answer to someone else. At this rate they'll never get back into the realm to save Max before something truly terrible happens to her … if it hasn't already.

They're having another 'meeting' this morning. Yesterday, after much argument, the officials decided that Jack and his team will be permitted to re-enter the gateway. The South African kids, on the other hand, all agreed that they'd had enough of the Realm, and would remain with their families and await Jack's team's return.

Much was talked about in that conference, and everything was meticulously recorded. Each of the kids had a turn in relaying their experiences, and slowly, but surely, the taskforce managed to get a clearer picture of what they were up against.

Today's discussions are once again being held at the hospital since Jack hasn't had his clearance to leave yet. There's a lot of tension in the room, mainly from the parents. Kenny's family are adamant that they won't be letting him go back in there, and this sets off the other parents in protest. The situation becomes so loud and heated that the deputy director general asks the kids to temporarily leave the room so that he can try to cool down the situation.

They wait in the corridor just outside.

'I knew it,' Kenny says miserably. 'Trust my family to be the cats amongst the pigeons.'

'Man, remind me to never get on your mum's bad side.' Peanut laughs. 'She's scary!'

'Tell me about it. Why do you reckon I get my brother to lie for me most of the time? She's so OTT! You do realise that I'm grounded until I'm twenty-five, don't ya?'

They laugh at poor Kenny's dilemma.

'Look,' Jack says, suddenly serious, 'hear me out for a sec. I know the deputy said he's going to settle things down in there, but what if he's only playing us?'

'What do you mean?' Ruby asks.

'Who's to say he's not just stringing us along. You know, telling us what we want to hear, but really only getting us on side so we can be more co-operative, and then later conveniently reneging on his promise when push comes to shove?'

Peanut laughs. 'Come on, Jack, now you're being paranoid. Ya reckon he'd do something sneaky like that?'

'Well, listen to them. Can you hear anything?'

They stop, silent. There's no yelling, nor is there the sound of any type of dispute on the other side of that door. Peanut's smile vanishes.

'You're right, Jack; it's too quiet,' Kenny says, his expression darkening.

'I know I'm right. If I've learnt anything from our time in that place, it's to trust no one. I reckon they're pulling a swiftie!'

The four friends look at each other in alarm.

'Look,' he tells them, 'I reckon we'll know if they're up to something the second we go back in there.'

'Yeah, just look at my mum. If she's smiling, then we'll know for sure.' Kenny chuckles without humour.

'So we need to come up with a plan B.' Ruby's eyes brighten with excitement.

Peanut's eyes narrow. 'I don't get you, Rubes. Why the sudden eagerness to go back?'

'To tell you the truth, it's gnawing at me that we're sitting around and not doing anything. Max needs our help—like she needs it yesterday. What part of that don't they get? It's as though they've got to go over everything a million times before anything gets done. I'm sick of hearing that we need clearance for this and clearance for that.'

'Same,' Jack says. 'This waiting is driving me nuts!'

'Let's take back some of that control,' Kenny says with enthusiasm. 'Like Ruby said, we should come up with a plan B, just in case.'

'So what should we do?' Ruby asks.

Jack smiles. 'I've been racking my brain trying to come up with something, and I reckon I've finally got just the thing. But man, I should've thought of doing this sooner,' he shakes his head in frustration, 'because we've missed a few crucial opportunities already.'

Jack runs his idea by them, and they quickly catch up to speed on his thinking. Soon the gang have found a direction and, more importantly, are coming up with ideas of their own to form a solid plan.

The conference door opens, and Gerard Thompson asks them to re-enter. Four pairs of eyes go straight to Kenny's mum … and surprise, surprise, Mrs Chen is sporting the biggest smile of them all.

PARANOIA

JACK

Jack questions his earlier paranoia as they trek through the national park, re-tracing their steps to the gateway to the Ancient Realm. Up ahead is the taskforce unit, headed by Captain Dean Logan, followed closely by Ryker's dad, Vice Admiral Engelbrecht, and Max's dad, Dr Rutherford. And at the rear walk half a dozen armed men and women as well as paramedics and SES workers. Jack is surprised to see such a large contingent—about twenty of them altogether. He realises now why it's taken them so long to get their act together. Of course, they won't all be entering; some will remain and set up camp this side of the gateway, ready for whatever may eventuate.

He takes a moment to readjust his heavy backpack and turns to make sure that Ruby, Peanut and Kenny are managing okay behind him. They look just as eager as he is to get back in there.

He's thankful that they were able to leave without any last-minute hysteria from the parents. Surprisingly, even Kenny's mum was on her best behaviour, which at first did make him a little suspicious, but his doubts were finally put to rest when his father made a last-ditch effort to change his mind. It wasn't anything he said, just the way he held his son when saying his last good-byes. His father pulled him into a tight hug and held him for several minutes, then he looked him in the eye, with tears threatening to spill, and without saying a word, walked away.

But now, although confident that his paranoia was a figment of his imagination, his father's behaviour, and the fear he saw in his eyes just before letting him go, makes Jack seriously question what they're about to do. *But it's different. This time we've got the military behind us. It'll be okay.* He shakes off his unease and moves ahead.

They cautiously make their way through the forest, knowing that there are still two realm guards roaming the national park somewhere. According to the media, apart from a couple of random 'sightings,' the military have had no luck in tracking them down.

'I wonder what happened to them,' Jack says to Peanut. 'It's like they've vanished off the face of the earth.'

'They've probably gone back. Why would ya hang around here?'

'Ya reckon? Even with all the security out here?'

Peanut shrugs.

The military presence makes itself known as they approach the ravine. Soldiers carry out formal security checks, thoroughly scanning and verifying everyone's ID. Once that's done, the portal site becomes a hive of activity with the setting up of the campground. Jack finds the building of the first-aid tent most impressive. He watches the team of doctors and paramedics jump into action, systematically converting a bare patch in the forest into a medical emergency centre. Although amazed with the quick and smooth setup, Jack hopes it'll never be needed.

He notices that an area adjacent to the camp has also been cleared to allow a helicopter to land. Everything appears to be thought of with meticulous organisation. Nothing has been left to chance. This comforts him. He's becoming more and more impressed with what measures have been taken to make this mission a success.

Captain Logan calls the company to attention

in preparation for the infiltration. He starts to run through a few final details.

Jack's heart starts to race. The time to enter is fast approaching. He looks towards the gauzy veil with a little apprehension but quickly shakes it off.

'Hey, are you guys ready?' he asks his friends as he removes his backpack to listen to the final instructions. The others do the same.

'Mate, with all this back-up, how can we go wrong?' Peanut chuckles. 'I say bring it on. Those ancients won't know what's hit 'em. I can't wait to show these guys what we can do. Rubes, are you ready? Man, they're gonna love you.'

Ruby leans over and gives Peanut a kiss on the cheek. And, just like that, Peanut's freckles vanish into the blush of his face.

Jack laughs. That 'bigger picture' Peanut always talks about suddenly got a whole lot more real. 'Hey, Kenny, you okay?'

'Sure. All for one, and one for all! I'm just thankful my parents backed off in the end.' He grins. 'I'm with you, Peanut. Look at all of this reinforcement. We'll all be back here, safe and sound, before you know it.'

All four stand silently listening to Captain Logan, oblivious to what's going on behind them. Suddenly, Jack is apprehended in an arm lock. 'What the hell!' He turns in a panic and sees that soldiers have also grabbed his friends. He can't believe it. They've been double-crossed! He struggles against the restraints. 'Hey, what's going on?'

'Guys, I'm afraid this is unavoidable,' Logan tells them. 'We've been given our orders from higher up. Jack, you and your friends will remain here while the taskforce complete their duty.'

'What are ya doing? Are you all insane?' Peanut yells at him. 'Don't you get it; you need us!'

'No, Peanut, it's you that doesn't get it. This situation is highly dangerous. We can't risk you getting hurt. Look, you've all been extremely co-operative, and the information that you've given us has been vital, but we won't be allowing you to come any further … I'm sorry, but it needs to be this way.'

Jack looks from the captain to the vice admiral and then to Max's father, silently pleading for their support on this. But they're clearly unified against them. It kills him to know that he was right. He should've followed his gut instinct.

Ruby suddenly lets out a terrifying scream. Jack turns, ready to protest that they're unnecessarily manhandling her when he sees what she's seeing—the two missing realm guards running straight at them.

All of a sudden, several things happen at once: the soldiers let go of their hold in order to arm themselves; Jack dives onto Ruby and pulls her to the ground with him; Kenny throws himself down, next to them, and the squad move into formation, ready for action.

But Peanut runs towards the portal.

The soldiers take aim, ready to shoot down the guards, but Captain Logan cries out, telling them to hold back in case they hit the civilian.

They watch in disbelief as Peanut throws himself at the guards, attempting to block their entry into the realm, but all he succeeds in doing is ricocheting off of them and into the portal.

The guards dive through, directly after him.

21

WHAT DO I DO NOW?

PEANUT

Peanut struggles to free himself from the vice-like grip on his ankle. He then remembers that he can vanish, so he does. He kicks wildly at the hand on his ankle—there's no way he's going to get caught—and he eventually manages to loosen his captor's hold by booting him firmly in the face. After a few more debilitating blows, the guard relinquishes his prisoner.

Peanut doesn't stop to consider anything, just wanting to get as far away from the two guards as possible. But mid-escape he realises he should remain close-by the portal in case the squad enter straight after him. Then he remembers their treachery. *Those sneaky, double-crossing, two-timing rats. Why should I help them? I should just let them get caught so they know what it feels like to be trapped here!*

But he can't do that. He wouldn't do that to Max; she needs them to help her get out.

He takes a moment to slow his rapid breathing, and then quietly makes his way back to wait for them. He positions himself behind a large boulder, convincing himself that the extra cover will give him added protection. And then he remembers … *For crying out loud; you're invisible, ya twit!*

He curses himself for being so stupid sometimes. And then he inwardly moans when he calls to mind what he'd just done to get him in this predicament in the first place. *What the hell was I thinking taking on those guards?* He shakes his head, unable to explain that knee-jerk reaction. The snipers had them in their sights, and now he's gone and stuffed it all up. That realisation makes him determined, now more than ever, to set things right somehow.

He waits for his friends to pass through and watches the two guards pick themselves up off the ground. The one that had him by the leg swipes away the blood from his broken nose. Peanut prepares himself. He looks around, anxious to see if there's anything nearby that he can use when the time comes. He spots a broken tree limb that might come in useful, and runs through a plan in his mind.

His attention returns to the wavering veil, wondering what's taking them so long. And then he hears a familiar thrashing sound that, if he's not mistaken, signals the approach of the portal guards. By re-entering the realm, they've triggered some kind of alarm.

The two guards hear it, too, and immediately appear nervous.

Within seconds Peanut sees that his hunch is right. A group of five brawny guards appear. Peanut recognises them from the first time they entered the realm all those months ago. The only one missing is Herodus.

'Marcus, Atticus, explain your absence?' one says. 'We have been scouring the forest in search of you. Herodus is livid.'

'Artemius, we have only just returned from the other world. They are planning an attack. We must prepare ourselves.'

'What is this?'

The second guard fills them in. 'In our attempt to apprehend the escapees, we found ourselves lost in their world. It is only by chance that their return to the gateway is cause for us to find our way back providentially. And there are many, with unfamiliar weapons, prepared to invade and conquer as we speak. One of them has already entered.'

'Quick, we need reinforcement.' The head guard calls forward one of his men. 'Miltiades, go at once and warn Herodus. And bring back with you any Invincible he can spare. Hurry!'

Peanut watches in horror as the guard takes off. He's got to do something.

His heart starts pounding in a panic. He tries to calm himself so he can think straight. And then, miraculously, he has a light-bulb moment; he'll take off after the guard and knock him out, that way preventing that message from getting delivered. *Genius!* But before he acts on it, he realises that if he does, he'll be abandoning his post and potentially sealing the unit's fate when they enter. *What do I do?*

One second he's ready to take flight, the next, he's resolved to remain and be on hand to warn the others. He feels too much pressure to make the right move, and his indecisiveness causes his head to spin. Precious time is being wasted. He hunkers down, suddenly feeling light-headed, and takes in a few deep breaths. *Get a grip!*

He finally decides to remain.

Movement from within the bushes nearby alerts him of another presence. Once again, his heart starts thumping erratically. The sound of a soft footfall to the other side of him puts him on high alert. And then, as though his heightened senses have made him aware of every discernible change around him, he sees something that makes his stomach drop. Forest people completely surround him, and amongst them is the savage that skewered him with his spear not that long ago.

Before impulsively making a run for it and blowing his cover, he remembers he's invisible. All he needs to do is remain quiet.

But the small man makes his way straight towards Peanut as if he were visible to him. This takes his panic to a whole new level. Peanut thinks back to their last encounter. *He couldn't see me then, so what's changed? Surely, he can't see me now!* He takes in a shaky breath and tries to calm himself down.

With incredible stealth, the man inches closer and closer, almost until he's on top of Peanut, and then he stops. 'Reveal yourself,' he whispers, 'for I know of your presence.'

Peanut's heart almost gives out on the spot.

22

CHANNEL EIGHT

JACK

Jack watches Peanut vanish through the portal. He races towards the diaphanous curtain in horror, but is tackled to the ground in seconds. 'What the hell! Let me go!' He kicks against the hold the soldier has on him.

Kenny runs to his aid, ramming the task-force member to throw him off. But Captain Logan is quick to react and gets Kenny in an arm lock before he has a chance to recover.

'What's going on here?' Ruby yells.

'Enough of this madness!' Captain Logan orders. 'You kids need to settle down, right now. I mean it! You're jeopardising this whole mission with these stupid reactions. That stunt Peanut just pulled was reckless, and not to mention, extremely dangerous.'

'He was only trying to stop the guards,' Ruby cries out.

'He nearly got himself killed,' he roars at her. 'And who knows what's happened to him now? For all we know he's already dead on the other side of this thing.'

His tactlessness makes Ruby sob inconsolably.

'Back off, Logan!' Jack shrugs off the soldier to go to Ruby's side. 'What did you think we'd do? Sit back and cop that blind-side on the chin? Respect and co-operation work both ways, you know, and right now I'm telling ya, you've gone and lost ours.'

Ryker's father steps forward. 'Jack, your loyalty is commendable, but reactions like this can, and will, lead to our downfall. This is exactly the reason why we've made this decision to leave you kids behind. We had it all under control; those guards were an easy target, but Peanut got in the way and foiled that.'

'Try to see what they're telling you here,' Max's father adds. 'Jack, your time in that place has triggered a basic, primitive or animalistic behaviour—to protect at any cost. These people here have been highly trained to be above that, to think and respond with logic and calculation.'

'What? You think we all react the way Peanut

does?' Jack snorts. 'True, he's a bit of a loose cannon, but none of us are like that. And I guarantee you,' he looks Captain Logan square in the eye when he says this, 'Peanut is not dead! That guy's a cat with nine lives. He lands on his feet no matter which way he's thrown. He's probably on the other side of this, waiting for us. So stop wasting time, and let's get on with it.'

The vice admiral looks ready to get into another row with him, but Jack gets in first. 'Oh, and before you try to shut me down again, I'm just gonna put to you exactly why we're coming. It might save us all a bit of time.' He gestures for Kenny to take centre stage.

Kenny awkwardly begins their argument. 'Um, so, this is what I've been doing the whole time we've been here.' He reaches into his front shirt pocket and unclips an electrical device concealed there. He holds it up for everyone to see. 'This is your average button camera that you can pick up on line for about two hundred bucks ...' He pulls out his phone, connects the device to it as he talks, then casually presses a few buttons and continues, '... and I've just downloaded the contents of what I've recorded onto a file, ready to send.' His finger hovers over the phone, waiting for Jack's say-so.

'What Kenny is trying to say,' Jack continues, 'is

that we've recorded everything that's been happening, from the meetings, to the strategies, to the agreements. Now we didn't want it to come to this, but you've left us with no choice. This mission back into the Realm … well, we're coming, and you're not gonna tell us otherwise, unless you want the whole world to know exactly what's been happening here. That reporter, you know, Trina Portabella from Channel 8 news, well, I'd say that she'd be pretty keen to hear from us right about now. What do you reckon?'

The repercussions of the media getting hold of a story like this would have the place swarming with reporters in no time. An exposed, secret portal from another dimension would become breaking news, and they all know it.

Jack holds back a triumphant smile when he sees the disbelieving look on the faces of the task-force leaders. *Checkmate.* 'Okay, I'm glad we've got that all cleared up, and we're back on the same page. Now, this is what's gonna happen …'

23

ONE STEP AHEAD

RYKER

Ryker stirs, but a sharp, stabbing pain in the head seizes him. His eyes clamp shut, and with great effort, he holds himself frozen in place, trying to avoid any further movement. He feels and smells straw beneath him. His stomach drops—everything is all too familiar.

He braces himself before opening his eyes a fraction, and from the thin slits, he can see that it's still night. The only discernible light comes from the cloudless sky outside. He turns slightly to face the window. A moonbeam spears his already sensitive eyes, causing him to wince and roll carefully out of its path.

The aspect from the barred window tells him he's returned to his former chamber. He can't tell yet if this is a good or bad sign. Does it mean he's once again a prisoner? Time will tell. At least he's within the fortress walls, and at the moment, that'll do.

The blow to his head has drained Ryker of his strength. He struggles just to keep his eyes open, let alone keep his thoughts in order, and so allows himself to find solace in a deep and restful sleep.

Sometime later, a bucket of cold water dowsed over his head jolts Ryker awake. He splutters from the water and the shock.

The sound of laughter only adds to the insult. 'Will you sleep the entire morn? I am surprised by your tardiness. Now, get up!'

'Oh my God, are you okay?' A familiar voice draws Ryker's attention. He shakes his head, this time oblivious to the stabbing pain.

'No, don't move. I've come to help.'

'Max, are you all right?' He reaches out for her and pulls her into an embrace. 'Tell me if they've hurt you, and I'll kill them!'

'Well, well, well; how touching. Tell me not, Ryker, but I feel that you have developed a fondness for our healer since we last spoke,' Herodus teases.

Ryker's heart stops. That unchecked outburst may have just cost them. He's revealed too much, but it's too late.

Herodus continues to laugh. 'Perhaps now you will be a little more willing to do my bidding.'

Ryker refrains from reacting. It's killing him to do it, because he's itching to belt that smug look from Herodus' face. 'What do you want?'

'Oh, a little touchy, are we? Then I will tell you plainly, for I see that you are not a man to be trifled with. It has been decreed that the games will recommence. And if I am correct in my knowledge, this will come into being sooner rather than later.'

Ryker's senses flick onto high alert.

'I see that this news comes as a surprise to you,' the head gate keeper taunts. 'The town's constructors have been labouring all hours of the day, repairing the arena in preparation.' He looks at Ryker before continuing, 'As it happens, we are in need of a replacement for Beowulf, and since your friends are responsible for his death, you have been chosen for the undertaking of it.'

Ryker bites back a triumphant grin—his plan has worked. But he can't afford to be too confident. 'Chosen? And what if I say no? I've been trying to get away from you for four years, what makes you think that I'll agree to this delusion of yours?'

'Ryker, you surprise me. The choice to take up the offer is entirely yours, my friend. But perhaps you will allow me to make your decision an easy one.' Herodus yanks at Max's arm, causing her to cry out in pain, 'How well do you care for your healer friend?'

'You touch her and I promise you'll regret it!'

'As you see, the decision rests entirely in your hands. Do as I say, and I shall hold you in favour. But decline the offer …' he starts to laugh, '… well, let us simply say that the choice you make will ultimately steer the outcome of your friend's future. And I am certain that you do not wish to be responsible for her demise, do you now?'

'No, Ryker, don't do it. I'll be okay,' Max cries out.

'Silence!' Herodus strikes Max across the face. The impact of the blow throws her up against the wall. She falls to the ground, her mouth and nose smeared with fresh blood. 'You will speak only when you are spoken to!'

Suddenly out of control, Ryker dives for Herodus, desperate to snap his neck in half. But two massive guards grab him and hold him back. His throbbing head prevents him from fighting them off.

'What say you, then?' Herodus demands. 'For my patience is wearing thin. If we are to come to an agreement, your training will commence immediately.' Herodus smiles another sinister smile. 'Friend against friend … that should make for some interesting entertainment, would you agree?'

Ryker's heart jolts.

'Again, you look surprised, my friend.' He chuckles. 'Do not think I am ignorant to what transpires in the woods. Remember this … I am, and always will be, one step ahead of you. Always!'

Herodus knows too much. And although Ryker's plan to become the reluctant volunteer has worked, this new development has him worried. He needs to agree to do this so he can protect Max. This makes his decision an easy one. As for the other problem, he'll need to find a way to tackle that later.

'What say you?' Herodus repeats, his tone impatient.

'You have me strategically cornered, so I have no choice.'

Herodus grins, revelling in the victory.

Before leaving, he throws Max to the ground, 'Now fix him, for he has work to do.'

The guards release Ryker and follow Herodus out, bolting shut the door behind them.

Ryker dissolves into a heap on the floor, and Max falls to his side and starts to cry. 'Oh, Ryker, I thought you were dead.'

'Hey, shh, look at me … as you can see, I'm not dead,' he says, trying to console her. 'But are you okay? I'll kill them if they've hurt you.'

'Don't worry about me; I'm good.'

She says this, but he can see the dark shadows under her eyes and knows she hasn't slept. And from the looks of the way her new clothes sit on her bony body, she hasn't been eating either.

'Tell me what's happening,' she asks eagerly. 'Have we had any word from Jack and the others? How did you get caught?'

Ryker explains everything while Max busies herself fixing his fractured skull.

'What! You deliberately got caught?' Her surprise turns to anger. 'Why would you do that? All you had to do is wait for them to come back. What's going to happen now that you're in here, too?'

'I'm going to look after you, that's what. Look, I needed to know you were okay, and from what I can see, I'm glad I came. No offence, Max, but you look like crap.'

This stops her ranting. She lets out a frustrated breath, then punches him playfully in the arm. 'Geez, don't hold back. Why not tell me what you really think?'

He smiles. 'Hey, I'm just keeping it real.'

'Wow, you really know how to make a girl feel good about herself, don't ya?'

He reaches out, takes her laughing face into his hands and looks deeply into her eyes for a moment.

Something's changed, but he can't quite work out what. And just like that, his thinking is scrambled.

Max breaks their gaze and looks away. 'I'm sorry, Ryker; I must sound ungrateful. I'm okay; really I am.' She tries to sound convincing, but he knows better. 'Hey, how's Aelianna, is she okay?' she asks in a sudden panic. 'I had to get word out to Medwin that I was still alive, and she was my only hope. Tell me she didn't get into trouble.'

Ryker's heart skips a beat at the mention of Aelianna's name. 'She's been amazing, Max. She's been pivotal in our planning. But we made sure she wasn't implicated in the set up. You don't need to worry; I'm positive she's safe.'

'So who's helping? You mentioned "we."'

'Medwin has been a great help, so has Alger, you know, the guy with the broken arm that you fixed.' He begins to tell her how the plan came about, but then notices her struggling to keep her eyelids open. She needs to rest now more than he needs to heal. 'Hey, I'm good now,' he lies.

'Really? I could've sworn I've a way to go still. Anyway, I'm amazed that you were functioning at all,' she says, stifling a yawn. 'Your head was a mess, but after what that creep did to you, I'm not really surprised.'

'Herodus knows too much. Do you think it was

Slade that squealed?'

'It has to be.' She lies down on the straw and, with her eyes half closed, continues in a mumble, '… before they took him away, he yelled that he knew stuff worth their while knowing. He must've been at that meeting and heard the plans.'

'That's not good. Jack and the others will be here any day now,' he says with dread. 'Let's hope they get past the guards without any problems. Until then we keep our noses clean and do what they want us to do. What do you think?'

'Hmm …' she mumbles, half asleep.

He gently brushes aside a strand of hair that's fallen over her face and tucks it behind her ear. 'My poor Maxine, what have they done to you? Sleep tight, little one. I'm here now.' He places a soft kiss on her temple, then lays down alongside her, tucking her in tightly against his chest. They sleep.

24

WHAT THE ...

RYKER

The door flies open, and Ryker wakes with a start. He must've dosed off for a minute. Two guards barge in and yank Max to her feet.

'What the hell are you doing!' He tries to stop them from dragging her away.

But one of the guards draws a large knife from his belt and holds it to Max's throat. 'Step back! I will not hesitate to slit her throat if you come any closer.'

Max's eyes bulge at the threat. 'It's, it's okay, Ryker. Keep your nose clean, remember?' she reminds him.

Ryker backs off. 'But she's weak. She needs to rest.'

'She has work to do. And as for you, you have

been summoned for your demonstration.'

Demonstration?

The guards motion for them both to exit the chamber. They take them straight to Herodus, where another guard ushers Max away.

'How do you expect her to function like this?' Ryker again tries to reason with Herodus.

Herodus charges at Ryker and looks him threateningly in the eye. 'She is responsible for this carnage, so she will fix it. This does not concern you.'

Ryker pushes him out of his face. 'She's useless to anyone the way she is. She can barely hold herself upright.'

'I have been given my orders, and unlike you, I do not question them.' He stares with such loathing after Max as she disappears down the passageway that Ryker's concern for her safety hits the roof.

What the hell was that look? What's he going to do to her?

Herodus loses himself in thought so deep that he appears to forget where he is.

Whatever has Herodus looking so tortured all of a sudden sends Ryker into a panic. 'Look, I'll do anything you want, I promise. Just let her go. Don't hurt her.'

Herodus snaps out of his reflections. 'She is Eshmun's responsibility,' he yells with excessive aggression. 'You, on the other hand, are mine. And for both our sakes, you need to present well before The Ancients. And I warn you, if you do not, I will personally see to it that your friend suffers for your insolence.'

Ryker's blood goes cold. The threat to Max makes him ready to rip the man's throat out and beat him to a pulp. But he doesn't. With a Herculean effort, he holds back and reins in his hatred for him, knowing that if he doesn't, he'll more than likely sign Max's death sentence.

Keep your nose clean.

His hands are well and truly tied. What was he thinking? His being here hasn't helped Max in the least. He can only pray and hope that their new friend, Aelianna, might be able to keep her safe, somehow.

Herodus leads Ryker through the passageways and into the arena. It's now the late hours of the afternoon. The sky is streaked with hues of orange and red, signalling the end of a day.

Ryker sees for the first time the devastation made by the elephant stampede. He's in awe of the genius behind such a catastrophe. *A few fire crackers and a basket full of mice made this mess.* He grins to himself. *That mind of Kenny's is a weapon in itself.* He smiles as he thinks back to their challenges. *They really did have the perfect team.*

Herodus marches Ryker past the hive of activity of the construction towards a section of the stadium that hasn't been ruined. Ryker sees the nobles seated there overlooking the arena. Pius, looking very much alive, sits in the centre of the group.

Distracted by the scene in front of him and wondering how it could be remotely possible for the games to continue, Ryker doesn't see, until they're almost upon him, the two burley guards wielding knives that suddenly charge at him. He instinctively goes into defensive mode.

One of the guards lashes at him, but Ryker disarms him with a swift high kick, then grabs his assailant and punches him square in the face. Almost simultaneously, he swings around to disarm the second attacker with a well-placed kick to the stomach. Another guard comes from behind and grabs Ryker in a neck hold. Ryker throws this third attacker over his shoulder and knocks him out cold with a direct blow to the head. The other two guards regroup and circle him with knives in hand. Wasting no time, Ryker grabs the one closest to him, punches the knife from his hand, then uses him as a battering ram to knock down the other. He pounces on them both, smashes their heads together and leaves them motionless on the ground.

Ryker turns at the sound of applause.

Pius stands before him, clapping slowly with appreciation. 'An impressive exhibition. Herodus, you have chosen well.'

'I am grateful for your approval, My Lord.'

'He has the strength of a bull, and the reflexes of a panther. Have him ready for the challenges. My recuperation has exhausted my interests. I do so desire some entertainment. I anticipate that our gateways will soon provide this?'

'Any day, My Lord.'

Ryker's heart skips a beat. He needs to warn Medwin that they're onto them. Jack and the others will need all the help they can get. They mustn't get caught. There's no way he's going up against one of his friends in a challenge—no way in the world.

'Oh, and of course,' Pius calls out before they leave, 'Herodus, we shall await your return for tonight's ceremony to begin.'

Herodus' disposition instantly alters. 'As you wish, My Lord,' he replies through clenched teeth.

This reaction surprises Ryker. In all the years, he's never seen any derision towards the elders. Clearly Herodus isn't agreeable with their every command. He tucks that bit of information away for later.

Herodus grudgingly walks Ryker back into the labyrinth of passageways under the stadium. But this time they take a detour away from the old, mouse-infested chambers and head into an area Ryker has never seen.

'You will remain here, amongst the guards and your peers,' Herodus informs him, 'and I trust that you will not abuse this privilege.'

Ryker follows, deep in his own thoughts. A petite, doe-eyed, female servant passes him in the corridor. He does a double-take and realises that it's Aelianna. He's so surprised to see her that he fails to guard his reaction.

Herodus, with his sharp eye, misses nothing. 'She is a beauty; I grant you that.' He then leans in and says quietly, 'But you would be wise to keep your hands to yourself where she is concerned. I have heard that her husband is one of the most savage forest people that you will ever have the misfortune to encounter. He is as big as a mountain and can snap a man in half like a twig.'

Initially Ryker breathes a sigh of relief, thankful that Herodus misinterpreted his look of surprise at seeing Aelianna as one of interest. But, strangely, his world simultaneously tilted sideways on hearing, once again, that she has a husband. *Did Medwin get it wrong?* His heart sinks.

Herodus interrupts his thoughts. 'Your training will begin at first light. I leave you now to attend to another matter. Rest well, for the schedule that I have prepared will challenge even the likes of you. And since the need for your services will present itself soon, I expect you to be prepared.'

Herodus leaves, closing the door behind him. Ryker listens, expecting to hear the door being bolted from the outside, but it's not. After a few minutes, he cautiously tries the door and is surprised to find it unlocked. He smiles at that unexpected discovery. *Keep your nose clean*, he reminds himself, and decides to stay put.

He looks around the room and is surprised to see that it's fitted with a few things that he's been without these last four years—a bed, a table and chair, as well as a washbowl. He lies down on the bed and revels in its softness, then closes his eyes and lets it all sink in. After four years of sleeping on a straw-covered, dirt floor, the bed feels like sheer bliss.

He remains there, going over everything that's happened today. His heart breaks a little when he thinks of Max. She's far worse-off than what he'd imagined, or even what she'd led him to believe. The dark shadows under her eyes and loose-fitting clothes told him a different story. He needs to find a way to help her. *But how?*

His stress levels shoot through the roof as he wrecks his brain to come up with something. He needs to come up with a plan before it's too late.

25

The White Tunic

Max

The thug assigned to getting Max is brutal. Exhausted from Ryker's healing, she struggles to keep up with him, and he hauls her through the meshwork of corridors at such a pace that she wonders what the hurry is. The passageways are so narrow that in his carelessness he slams her against the walls, and he's either completely oblivious or doesn't care that she's getting a beating.

It surprises her that they're heading back in the direction of her chamber and not to the infirmary where hundreds of injured people are still waiting for her to help them. *Surely, Eshmun hasn't allowed me to have some time out?* But something's wrong; she can feel it in her gut. She starts to panic when she realises that she's alone with this guy … and he could be taking her anywhere.

She reminds herself that Herodus had once said that no one would dare touch her knowing that she was promised to him. Knowing this relaxes her a little, but her guard goes up again when they arrive at her chamber to find Aelianna waiting for her. Max looks warily around the room and sees that the tub is full of water and a small table loaded with soap, oils and lotions sits beside it. She turns to Aelianna, a question in her eyes, and notices a sharp metal utensil in her hand … something that looks like a pair of scissors.

Her heart starts racing. Max doesn't know what to think. Has she put her trust in this girl and now she's been betrayed? Did Herodus find out what they're up to and has ordered Aelianna to kill her to save herself?

'Max, do not alarm yourself! Come sit and catch your breath, for you look as though you are close to passing out.' Aelianna takes Max by the hand and gently guides her to the bed. Max notices a white tunic on the bed and something orange lying next to it—something that looks very much like a veil.

Max's eyes widen with sudden understanding. She jumps off the bed, runs to the corner of the room and slides down the wall to sit on her haunches. The word 'betrothal' echoes repeatedly in her head. She begins to hyperventilate.

'Max, are you well?' the fearful look on Aelianna's face reminds Max to breathe. Aelianna takes Max's face in her hands and looks deeply into her eyes. 'Max, we must hurry; the nobles are waiting. They are impatient for the ceremony to begin. And I dare not anger Herodus, either. He has been like a bear poked awake from his sleep.'

'Wha … what's going on?'

Aelianna squashes a smile. ''Tis your betrothal, silly.'

Max's gut clenches into a knot at the confirmation. She falls to the side and tries to vomit, but because she's had nothing to eat, her retches produce nothing but bile. It rises from her stomach to burn her throat and fill her mouth.

'Oh, had you forgotten? But I cannot be surprised, for you were barely awake when I gave you the news last eve.'

Max starts to see stars before her eyes, but before she passes out, Aelianna brings her some water to wet her lips. 'Now, not too much at first. Just a few sips until your colour returns.'

Max numbly does as she's told.

'I hate to ask you this, but we really must make haste.' Aelianna pulls her up to her feet and begins to undress her.

Oblivious to Aelianna's attentions, Max finds herself up to her neck in lavishly scented water, having her hair washed. She's told that the water has been blessed—holy water from a sacred fountain.

The warmth of the water lulls her into a state of calm, and it's not until, sometime after the bath, she sees Aelianna produce the scissors again that she snaps out of her tranquil state to realise what she's about to do with them. She puts her hand out to stop her. 'What are you doing?'

Aelianna looks at her, baffled. 'But, Max, it is customary to cut off the bride's hair before the ceremony.'

'No way!'

'But I must. It is expected.'

Max sees the terror in Aelianna's reaction. *God, they wouldn't hurt her because I didn't let her cut my hair, would they?*

Tears start to pool, then spill down Aelianna's cheeks. The look on her face tells Max clearly that they would. Max can't let that happen. She takes in a shaky breath, shuts tight her eyes and tells her to just do it. *It's just stupid hair, right. It'll grow back.*

The grinding sound of the blades as they hack at her long dark hair brings an unexpected sting to her eyes. As the tresses fall limp to the floor, she can't help but mourn their loss. And the pain pierces deeper still when she comes to realise the loss that's yet to come. Could this be the beginning of the end of her innocence?

26

AFTER THE CEREMONY

MAX

Max's heart races as she struggles to keep up with the guard taking her to Pius' chamber. She'd hate to think that Aelianna might get into trouble for them taking so long. They pause for a moment at the intricately carved wooden doors, waiting to be heralded in. Max gingerly touches the back of her head and tugs at the short strands. She thinks of her mother, remembering her beautiful long tresses, and bites back the tears threatening to fall.

'Enter!'

The doors swing open to reveal a small gathering.

The five nobles sit before her on their golden thrones with Pius seated in the centre. Eshmun stands to the side and, of course, Herodus is there. He stands with his back to her.

The guard shoves Max forward. She keeps her eyes lowered, desperate not to upset anyone, and stands beside the man who will soon be her husband. Herodus remains as cold and formidable as a stone statue. And then, unexpectedly, he kneels. She does the same. Her body trembles as the ceremony begins.

She feels sick to the stomach not knowing what's going to happen after this. Her thoughts race. She'll do anything if he just leaves her alone. She'll heal the injured without a word of complaint. She'll keep at it, day and night to save them all. She won't ask for water. She doesn't need a bed. She'll stay at the infirmary.

Tears start to fall. She can't stop them. At least the veil provides her with something to hide behind. But her sobs can't be so easily masked, and she struggles to hold back from crying.

She feels so bogged down with grief that she doesn't realise when the ceremony ends. It's only when Herodus stands and yanks her by the arm that she becomes conscious of it. Before she knows what's happening, she's trailing him down the corridor and heading for his chamber.

'Please! No!' She struggles against his grip on her wrist, but his hold only tightens as a result. 'Please, you're hurting me!'

They come to an abrupt halt outside his room. He yanks her towards him and glowers down at her.

Her heart feels as if it's jumped into her throat. She begs with her eyes for him to let her go, and then, miraculously, for reasons unknown, he does.

'Leave me. I need my sleep,' he snaps at her. 'You, on the other hand, need to get back to work. Eshmun will come for you shortly, so you would be wise to eat and rest before he comes.'

Speechless, Max stumbles backwards until she feels the door to her chamber at her back. She gropes behind her to push it open, then falls into the opened room. The last thing she sees is her husband slamming the door shut. She hears him bolt it from the outside. And then everything goes black.

27

RYKER'S NEW WORLD

RYKER

Ryker wakes early the next morning in a disorientated state, but the calming sounds of dawn outside his window reassure him. He sits upright and rubs at his eyes, not truly believing where he is, then laughs at himself when he realises that what he thought was a dream clearly wasn't.

He knows that he'll be called on soon, and that he'll be meeting with the Realm's champions, the Invincibles. This'll be the first time in four years that he's seen them. The last time, when they killed Jaeger, he was battling against them. His thoughts go back to that nightmare of a day making his blood boil and his stomach turn. But he can't allow his feelings about that to cloud what he's about to do here.

As expected, Herodus arrives to collect him moments after he finishes his meal. Ryker follows him through a maze of corridors until they reach an opening that leads to the outside. He's not familiar with the place. It's not the garden where he has spent the past four years, nor the arena. It's a market place. And in this bustling centre, he's surprised to see normal people going about their daily routine just like they would in any ancient village. People buy from stalls filled with goods. Kids play ancient games, stirring the dust on the ground, and dogs chase cats between the feet of the shoppers.

Ryker can't get his head around what he's seeing. He had no idea this normality existed in the Ancient Realm.

'Keep up!' Herodus bellows.

Ryker quickens his pace and soon enters a building that opens onto a large courtyard and pool. The four infamous Invincibles are there, reclining on couches near the water.

'I am here to advise you that the battle protocol has changed,' Herodus says, gaining everyone's attention. 'The Ancients have grown restless and have requested us to expedite the challenges. Therefore, you will battle the next innocent that enters the Realm. And I have it on good authority that it will be sooner rather than later. Therefore, I suggest you use your time well.' With that said, Herodus leaves.

The most senior of the champions, Athos, is the first to stand and greet him. 'So we meet again, young Ryker. I must say, you have captivated my interest from the day we first battled. From my extensive experience, your strength is second to none.'

Shant laughs. 'Oh, come now, Athos, the boy will develop a superiority complex if you do not take heed, and then where will we be?'

Ryker knows he needs to get them on side. 'I am truly humbled to be in your presence, Shant.' He then turns to the others. 'In all your presences.' He bows low to acknowledge each one of them, then turns back to the more intimidating of the four, Shant. 'Your performance in the recent battle has been much spoken of.'

The only female amongst them, Vyvian, looks delicate, almost ethereal, but her appearance is deceiving. She flies into the air and circles around Ryker, her eyes examining him with curiosity and admiration. Not missing her open interest in him, he bows even lower and indicates his approval of her with a sultry smile and a tweak of his brow.

'Oh, my!'

Ryker almost laughs. He congratulates himself on his performance. *That was too easy.* But then he suddenly feels faint, and his thoughts become muddled, almost painful. Before he turns to the obvious source of this—Archimedes, who has the ability to mess with people's minds—he silently starts singing the words of his favourite song, *Smells Like Teen Spirit* by Nirvana. The sensation of overwhelming negativity quickly vanishes. He then turns to the formidable Archimedes and acknowledges him once more with a discreet nod of the head.

The smug look on Archimedes' face vanishes.

'So,' Athos says, 'we have much work to do. There is talk that your adversaries from the last battle will soon be amongst us once again.'

'Good, I have a score to settle with them,' Ryker growls.

'This is remarkable,' Athos says with interest. 'We were under the impression that you have formed an attachment with their healer.'

Ryker shakes his head. 'Allow me to make clear that matter, once and for all. Perhaps there was a time where I did entertain some interest there.' He gives an arrogant smile. 'But she is a mere girl; what interest could she hold for a man when he is in the presence of a real woman.' He chances a glance at Vyvian, who appears flushed from the compliment.

Archimedes smiles. 'So it would appear that your tongue is as adept as your style.'

'Believe me,' Ryker says, sounding convincing to his ears, 'I don't take this honour given to me lightly. I'm determined to prove my worth and assure you that I have no interest but to battle alongside you, as an equal. I haven't the arrogance to consider myself as skilful as you yet, for I know that I've a lot to learn. My only wish is to one day be considered worthy of being part of this team.'

Archimedes peers through narrowed eyes at Ryker. 'I look forward to our future battles. Your actions in these matters may prove to speak louder than your words. Take heed, young Ryker, time will tell.'

That night, after a gruelling workout, Ryker falls exhausted on his bed. The Invincibles were relentless in their training and held nothing back. But Ryker, his will just as unyielding, hardened to the constant challenges, refused to be defeated. He kept repeating to himself that Max needed him and that his presence here means he'll somehow be able to protect her. But a concrete plan of action is still unclear in that regard. He lies there reminding himself that he needs to have faith and believe in timing and fate. As Medwin would say, 'The solution has not revealed itself because the time is not yet favourable.'

'Then I wish it would just hurry up and come, because I'm done with all this waiting!'

28

ᚼNCOUNTERING ᚼEDWIN ... ᚼGAIN!

PEANUT

'Reveal yourself!' the little man whispers again.

Peanut can't believe that he's been found out again. In a panic, his gaze darts around, looking for an escape. *What do I do?* With his pulse accelerating, he struggles to keep his breathing quiet. Silence is the only way of preventing this forest dweller from weeding him out.

The savage moves in a little nearer.

Sweat pours off Peanut's body.

To his horror, the man leans in closer still, and then whispers, 'Ryker needs you.'

189

Peanut startles, but the words were so softly spoken that he questions whether he's heard correctly. He decides not to answer.

The man leans even closer, his warm breath only centimetres away. 'Reveal yourself, for Ryker has sent me.'

Peanut can't believe it. This guy actually knows he's there. *How the hell is that even possible? And why would Ryker have sent this guy? No, it must be a trick.* He remains silent.

The small man, clearly frustrated, grumbles something unintelligible under his breath. And then in exasperation he whispers, 'Walnut? Almond? Now this is exceptionally ridiculous. Whatever your name is, Ryker is once again imprisoned and in need of your assistance.'

'How the hell did he get himself caught?' Peanut says, blowing his cover.

The small man nearly jumps out of his skin. He clutches at his chest as if traumatised. 'There is much to explain. Follow me.'

'I can't, my friends are coming. They'll be here any minute.'

'No, they will not. They will be detained.'

Say what! Peanut does a double-take.

'Remember, I once told you of my gift of foresight. Trust me, this is how I have come to be here this very moment. I saw you coming, and in my vision, you arrive alone.'

Peanut takes a moment to digest this. It all suddenly makes sense. And then his pulse accelerates when he realises what that means—Jack and the others have had a few more obstacles than what they anticipated. 'Then I've gotta stop the message getting to Herodus!'

'Your attempt to intervene will come to naught. I have seen this. Herodus will be notified and reinforcements will be sent. Our task is to save as many of your friends from capture as we can, for there will be imprisonment; this I have also foreseen. As to how many, well, this will be determined by the decisions we will now make.'

This is the worst news the man could've given Peanut. Somehow, he needs to stop Jack from re-entering, or at least warn them what's coming. His anxiety rises. He doesn't want to screw things up. 'So what do I do?'

'Come. While the guards are distracted by their own discussions, we will talk.'

Peanut follows the man as he carefully retreats into the forest. When they've reached a safe distance, Medwin stops, introduces himself and fills Peanut in on what's happened.

'Abducted? Again! Geez, poor Max.' The situation

is far graver than what Peanut imagined. 'And you say that Ryker got himself caught?'

'He needed to get within the fortress to protect her. Do not trouble yourself; no harm will come to her, for her gift is highly valued.'

They hear some movement up ahead, and it's drawing closer by the second. He and Medwin race back to their original hiding place and brace themselves for whatever's coming.

'I'm going to go back and warn them,' Peanut whispers. He turns to go, but Medwin blocks his path with his spear.

What the ...!

Medwin points at the portal in explanation. Peanut's gaze follows, and he sees the problem. The security there has doubled, and amongst the guards are Herodus and Shant, the Invincible. Peanut grimaces.

The transparent veil behind the guards starts to oscillate with renewed energy, forewarning them of an impending intrusion. The guards see this and stand ready.

Peanut jumps up from behind the boulder and shouts a string of nonsense words. The guards spin around, distracted by the ruckus. Medwin, following Peanut's lead, calls for the men hidden in the bushes to attack.

Armed with a broken tree branch, Peanut, in his invisible state, leads the assault. His first victim doesn't see what's hit him. He falls to the ground after receiving the full force of the limb to his face. Peanut doesn't stop. He prepares to swing at the next one, but the guard wises up, figuring out where Peanut is, and charges at him like an angered bull. Peanut drops his weapon and dives out of the way in time to save himself. He looks around for something else to use and sees the forest people in the thick of things, fighting off the guards with eager abandon. And then he notices that the portal is quivering faster, the movement gaining in intensity. He watches in alarm as Jack enters, followed by Ruby, then Kenny.

Peanut yells at them to run, but before they have a chance to take in what's happening, the guards pounce on them. Ruby gets knocked to the ground with such a force that she doesn't get back up.

'No!' Peanut dives onto the back of her attacker and starts beating him about the head. The guard struggles to throw him off, and once he has, Peanut searches for something to knock him out with. He sees a large rock and doesn't hesitate to use it on the guard's head. It hits with a sickening crunch and the man crumples to the ground. With that guard out of the way, Peanut falls to Ruby's side and tries to rouse her, but she's out cold. He pulls her into the forest to hide her, then looks up in time to see the other members of the taskforce stumbling through the gateway.

'Get the hell out of here!' he yells.

They get to their feet and prepare to attack - firearms raised, but a gale springs up around them, blowing so strong that the soldiers struggle to remain upright let alone maintain a firm hold of their guns. The wind snatches the weapons from their hands and flings them into the depths of the forest. The soldiers resort to knives and fists. Guards against soldiers in an all-in brawl.

Peanut sees that a guard has pinned Jack to the ground. He's struggling to fight off his attacker. Peanut doesn't think twice. He throws his whole body weight against the guard, knocking him off Jack, then he jumps on him and starts delivering punches.

Jack staggers to his feet and disappears, only to reappear moments later wielding a tree branch. He uses it to knock the guard out once and for all.

'Get Ruby out of here,' Peanut yells, pointing to where she lies. 'I'll keep them from coming after you.'

Jack races over to Ruby, picks up her unconscious body and makes a run for it.

Peanut looks around. Kenny needs help. The guard on top of him has him by the neck and is strangling the life out of him. Peanut grabs a huge rock that's lying nearby and smashes it against the guard's skull. The crunch he hears from the blow he delivers tells him that the man won't be getting up again soon.

Breathing hard, Peanut turns in time to see Shant raise his hands into the air ready to cause more havoc. Peanut dives in and tackles him to the ground, buying them a little more time.

But Herodus, whose keen eye misses nothing, retaliates. He races at Peanut and succeeds in grabbing him in a headlock. 'Shant, act now!'

Moments later a twister appears.

Peanut feels the stranglehold around his neck loosen somewhat and takes advantage. In one almighty thrust backwards, he manages to head-butt Herodus directly in the face. The man reels back, breaking his hold. Peanut dashes for the trees, yelling, 'Tornado! Run!'

People scatter into the forest in every direction.

Peanut stops running and stands, silent and still invisible, watching on in horror as Shant takes chase. He hears screams and cries for help as the rotating column of air vacuums up some of his friends. He only prays that Jack was able to get Ruby to safety in time.

Herodus shouts out his orders: four of his guards are to search for those that have fled into the forest;

two are to remain to protect the Gateway; and the rest are to follow him to assist Shant.

Peanut frowns, at a mental cross-road. Does he tail Herodus, find out the upshot of Shant's stunt and risk getting caught? Or does he stay put and help those left behind get away? He knows one thing for sure; he wants to be with his friends. But he's got no way of knowing where they are.

Herodus disappears into the forest, and Peanut makes his decision; he'll follow him. And if it happens that luck is on his side, he might be able to find out what happened to Max and Ryker, too.

29

CAT CRY

PEANUT

Peanut stays close behind the whirling tornado, his heart pounding uncontrollably as he nears the fortress. But the colossal, once-formidable stronghold somehow doesn't seem so indestructible to him now. The remnants of the damage they left behind is evident the moment he crosses over the drawbridge. Despite The Ancients' attempt to repair the damage, a large portion of the arena is still in complete ruins.

All construction comes to a halt as the workers become aware of the body of air swirling before them and the entourage closely following behind. They surge towards the spectacle, clearly welcoming the unexpected diversion. Peanut remembers the brutal challenges and the spectators' insatiable thirst for the macabre.

More guards run into the arena to assist.

'Once the captives are released from the windstorm, you will seize and imprison them,' Herodus tells them, his voice raised over the roar of the wind. 'They are to be taken to the challengers' chambers. There will be a need for them on the morrow.'

Oh my God! Don't tell me that they're gonna make them battle? And so soon? Peanut is devastated. Everything has gone wrong. He wasn't expecting anything like this to happen. *But against who? There's no one left to compete with.*

The guards circle Shant and wait at attention, distracting Peanut from his thoughts. He holds his breath as Shant slowly lowers the tornado's victims to the ground. Up until now, the ferocity of the whirling movement hasn't allowed Peanut to see who might be trapped within, but, to his horror, he catches a glimpse of a streak of long strawberry-blond hair. His blood goes cold.

He needs to come up with a way to stop this. He searches wildly for a plan of action. He needs a massive distraction, but what? *Where's Kenny when you need him? I'm sure he'd have no trouble coming up with something awesome.* And then his heart sinks when he realises that Kenny might be trapped in there, too. *What if I'm the only one that's escaped?*

He squats on his haunches to steady his sudden light-headedness.

When the funnel slows to a virtual stop, Peanut can see the reality of the situation. Ruby floats gently to the ground in her unconscious state. His heart sinks further when he sees that Jack is also amongst them. He falls protectively by her side. And De Beer and Gallo, two of the task-force soldiers, are in there with them.

It's killing him that he can't go to them. But then he realises that he can. At least he can let them know that he's there for them. He cautiously steps closer, but he needs to move quickly because they'll be taken away as soon as the dust has settled. But he's only just decided this when the guards close in on his friends and snatch their backpacks, leaving them with nothing but the clothes they're wearing.

De Beer and Gallo help Jack with Ruby before they begin the march. Two guards head the formation with another two at the rear. Peanut will surely be found out if he says anything now, so he resorts to making himself known to them by way of a cat cry—one he's confident Jack will recognise. So just before they're taken beneath the stadium, Peanut lets out the call. Jack stops, clearly recognising the familiar signal. The guard behind him shoves him forward and, thankfully, they continue without suspicion. Peanut watches them disappear into the labyrinth of passageways, relieved that he was able to make contact. What he needs to do now is figure out a way to help them get out.

But his attention diverts back to the arena when he overhears Herodus order one of his guards to take the backpacks to his private quarters. This prompts Peanut into action. His thoughts mull over a way to get his hands on those taskforce kits—they're packed with a whole heap of military gadgets.

Sick! If I can get my hands on some of the stuff in there, I'll have them out of there quicker than a scalded dog. Peanut feels ecstatic that he's come up with a plan. *… and it's a bloody good one at that!*

30

Which War Are We Fighting?

Jack

Jack can't believe it; Peanut is here. He'd recognise that cat cry anywhere. As kids growing up, they often used it to communicate with each other without anyone suspecting what they were up to. His relief is massive.

But then he looks down at poor Ruby. She's been out of it for a long time, and he's really starting to worry about her. He feels completely helpless.

I wish Max was here.

He tries his best to keep her comfortable by rolling up his jumper and placing it under her head.

He looks around – there's no water … no nothing; not a single thing he can do to make a difference.

'So you're pretty confident that your friend Peanut entered the fortress with us?' Lieutenant Gallo asks him as he paces back and forth, clearly trying to come up with a strategy.

'Quit it, Gallo. If the kid says he's sure, then he's sure,' the other soldier chews out.

'Back off, De Beer; there's nothing wrong with getting the facts right, okay?' the smaller of the two lashes back.

Jack has already had a gutful of these two. It's obvious they're on different camps even though they're supposed to be fighting the same war. And with the way Jack's feeling at the moment, he's not going to be able to put up with any more of their crap. His head throbs from the beating he got earlier, and there's not a spot on his body that isn't aching. He takes a moment to channel his power to help himself cope with the pain, then runs his hand through his blood-soaked hair and says, 'You guys need to pull your heads in, all right? We're in this thing together, so let's at least try to act like we're on the same team.'

The soldiers look at each other with obvious disdain but say nothing.

'So it looks like we're gonna compete in one of their stupid battles tomorrow,' Jack continues, 'and

I figure they'll pit us against their champions since they've got no one else for us to challenge. There's not that much time before dawn, so here's what's probably gonna happen …'

Although they've already been briefed on the Realm's defenders, Jack relays again what each of the Invincibles are capable of. He warns them about Archimedes in particular, and runs through the challenges they might come up against and what they need to do as a team to stay strong.

'Expect the unexpected,' he warns them. 'There might be wild animals and gladiator type fights, or it might be a team event. Although somehow I don't think so. Ruby would've been our trump card in any of those tasks. She's saved our arses heaps of times before, but we can't count on her this time, so—I'm not gonna lie—it's gonna be tough.' Jack rubs at his temples, suddenly overwhelmed. But then he realises that this talk of doom and gloom isn't doing them any favours, so he activates his inner calm again and projects it over them before they lose focus.

He then looks down at Ruby. 'I just hope she's all right. That jerk really slammed her hard.' He notices her eyelids start to flutter, as if she's struggling to open them. He kneels by her side and gently brushes her hair away from her face. 'Rubes, can you hear me? Hey, it's Jack; can you open your eyes?'

But her eyes stop twitching, and just like that, she's gone again.

'Psst!'

Someone's trying to get his attention from outside. 'Peanut?' He dives at the window, grabs the bars and hauls himself up to investigate. Gallo and De Beer join him in a flash. But, of course, they can't see anything.

'What the hell!' Peanut says. 'Is Ruby still out of it? Pry the bars apart so I can get in.'

Jack and the two soldiers fall back, alarmed by Peanut's outburst.

'Now!' he growls.

'Mate, there's nothing you can do,' Jack says, sending a blanket of calm over him. He needs to stop Peanut from totally losing it and giving himself away. His power soon has the desired effect.

'Ruby,' Peanut calls out to her quietly. 'Hey, Rubes, can you hear me?'

Her eyelids twitch again.

'Did ya see that?' Peanut cries out. 'She can hear me. Rubes, c'mon girl, you can do it.'

Jack falls to his knees and gives her hand a squeeze. Her eyes flutter some more, and then to everyone's relief, they open. She looks around the room, disorientated.

'She's awake! Babe, are you okay?'

'Peanut?' she searches anxiously for him.

'I'm here. Out the window. Thank God you're all right.'

Although Peanut remains invisible, his relief is obvious. And so is Jack's. He helps her up, but she struggles with obvious pain, so, without a second thought, he blankets her with all he has, and very quickly he notices her transformation.

'What happened?' she looks around the chamber, still not quite sure where she is, and then … 'For crying out loud, how did we end up back here?'

Peanut chuckles. 'Watch out, guys, she's ba-ack!'

Bracing himself for her reaction, Jack fills her in on what's been happening and, worse still, on what's to come.

'You mean to tell me we've got to compete again!' Ruby is livid. 'I'm so over this!' She turns to face the window. 'Peanut, you got us into this mess, so now you can just figure a way to get us out!'

'Hey, what's that supposed to mean?'

'What the hell were you thinking? Diving for those two guards?'

'Now, wait a minute …'

Jack steps between them before Peanut loses his head. He glares at them both.

Ruby purses her lips, and drops her tirade. Peanut lets out a submissive sigh.

'Right then, so what've you come up with?' he asks Peanut. 'Can you get us out of here?'

'I've just got back from trying to pinch back your back-packs—'

'Brilliant idea!' Gallo's expression lifts. 'How did you go?'

'Not so great. I followed the guard that took your gear, right up to where he was told to leave them, and then he bolted the door shut and plonked himself in front of it. And I can tell ya, he ain't going to budge anytime soon, that's for sure.'

'Maybe you should report back to Engelbrecht,' De Beer suggests. 'He could give you some explosives to blow us out of here.'

'Why Engelbrecht? Logan is in command,' Gallo challenges him.

'Engelbrecht outranks Logan, and you know it.'

'But we answer to Logan. And you know it!'

Jack sighs and stands between the two of them ready to smash their heads together. It's the Aussies versus the South Africans again, and the rivalry between them is wearing thin. His gaze shoots daggers at them.

Gallo gets the message right away. 'Right, okay, that's not such a bad idea after all, De Beer.'

Jack sighs, thankful to finally get a break. They don't have time for this sort of crap. He turns his attention back to what needs to be done. 'So, Peanut, do you reckon you've got enough time to get back before they come for us?' He can't imagine he has, but he gives Peanut a chance to answer the question himself.

'No,' Ruby says, 'it's too risky.'

Peanut remains quiet for a while before answering. 'Look, I'd like to say that it'd be a piece of cake, but to tell you the truth I don't think I'd make it. It's as black as the ace of spades out there, and knowing my luck I'd get lost and totally stuff things up.'

'Your best bet, then, is to get our stuff back. Is there another way of getting into that room? Because if there is, we've got explosives and night vision goggles in our kit,' Gallo tells him.

'Whoa … pyrotechnics on steroids. Awesome!'

That does it, right there. Jack knows Peanut has found his incentive to get past that guard.

'I could try getting into that room from the outside …' He sounds giddy with anticipation. 'I can't promise anything, but I'm starting to get my bearings around this place, so with a bit of luck maybe that's doable. Surely they don't have bars on Herodus' windows?'

Before anyone's had time to react to that, they hear him take off. 'So I'll be off. I'll catch ya later.'

And then he's gone.

31

'Who's Camp Are You On?

RYKER

Ryker is half asleep when he hears a rustling sound just outside his window. He snaps to attention and listens intently.

'Psst!'

He almost jumps out of his skin—someone's trying to attract his notice. He dives out of bed and peers out the small window. But he doesn't see anything except the darkness of night, so he turns away, certain he imagined it.

'Hey, it's me, Peanut!'

'What? Where are you?'

'Shh! I'm here, but keep it down, will ya.'

'You guys made it!' His heart pounds with excitement.

'Yeah, but everything's gone pear-shaped. Look, I don't have time to explain, but Jack and Ruby have been caught, and they're about to battle the Invincibles.'

His heart skips a beat. 'Yeah, I kind'a knew that something like this was gonna happen.'

'What? How?'

Ryker draws in a deep breath. How's he going to say this without Peanut totally getting the wrong idea? He starts from the beginning and relays what's happened as briefly as he can.

'I didn't know how long you guys would be, so I acted on what I thought was the best direction to take.'

He waits for Peanut's reaction but there's nothing but silence.

'Hey, are you still there?'

'So … nice set-up you've got here, *mate*. Looks like you've come up in the world.'

Ryker doesn't miss the sarcasm. 'Hey, what was I supposed to do? Max was in trouble, and I had to get in here to look out for her, okay? What's your problem?' He's burning right now. He can't believe how quick Peanut was to question his motives.

'Whoa … back off!'

'Back off? I stick my neck out, and this is what I get!'

'Okay, sorry. But how can ya blame me? From where I'm standing, this whole thing looks a little sus.'

Ryker looks around his room, tries to see what Peanut is seeing and realises what he means. 'Mate, I've been trying to get out of this place for four years. What makes you think I'd choose to stay here one second longer if I didn't have to?'

'Yeah, point taken. So …'

'So what?'

'What's gonna happen now? I mean, you're gonna battle against your mates, and from what I can gather, it'll be pretty soon.'

'They've got Ruby on board, right?'

'Yeah, lucky. She was knocked out for a while, but now she's come good.'

'Well, then the Invincibles won't stand a chance— like last time. But just warn Jack that they've become wiser, and they've got a different game plan.'

Ryker catches Peanut up to speed on what the challenge is, and what he thinks might pan out during the battle. And then they go over various counter-attacks that Jack should try.

Once done, Peanut leaves him to try his luck

getting into Herodus' chamber. Ryker prays he'll somehow find a way. But he doesn't hold much hope for him. If the window to his room is barred and as small as this one, then he's got no hope.

Ryker spends the last moments before they call on him to psych himself up for what's about to go down. He paces back and forth with a sickening knot in his gut, dreading what he's about to do. There's going to be a fine line between revealing his true alliance and getting the job done—after all, he still needs to protect Max.

32

Chummy With The Enemy

Jack

Peanut has been gone for a while now. Jack paces back and forth, unable to settle down. De Beer and Gallo have already crashed. He wonders how on earth they can just switch off like that.

'Jack, you're making me nervous. Sit down,' Ruby says, exasperated.

'Sorry. Hey, are you okay?'

'What? Since the last time you asked me two minutes ago?' she laughs. 'Jack, relax. You've got to learn to trust what Peanut's doing.'

'It's not that I don't trust him; I'm just worried

that he might get caught. Remember what they did to him the last time?' The moment the words come out, Jack regrets saying them. 'No, Ruby, I didn't mean that. I'm such an idiot. I'm sorry.'

The sound of a cat call from outside has him spin around and dive to the window.

Ruby is there just as quickly. 'Is that him?'

'Yeah, gorgeous, it's me.'

She pulls herself up to the window and leans in to get a kiss from her invisible boyfriend.

'Hey, cut it out.' Jack laughs with relief. 'So what's the go?'

Peanut groans. 'Oh, man, I don't know where to start. What do ya want to hear first, the bad news or the worse news?'

De Beer and Gallo stir from the commotion and sit up, suddenly very alert.

Jack's gut clenches. 'Okay, let's have it.'

'So I found Herodus' chamber, but he's got iron bars on the window just like these ones. Go figure. And even if I could somehow manage to budge them, and believe me, I tried, there'd be no way in hell I'd fit through that tiny opening.'

Jack is gutted. 'Was that the *worse* news?'

'Um … nah, sorry,' he tells them reluctantly, 'brace yourselves … that's coming now.' Peanut pauses a moment to let out a deep and devastated breath. 'D'ya remember Medwin - you know the guy that speared me in the foot? Well, I came across him just before you guys got caught. I know I didn't tell you this, I kind'a forgot. Well, anyway, he told me that while we were away, Ryker got himself caught so he could get back into the fortress and somehow protect Max.'

'Are you trying to tell us that you've found Ryker?' De Beer says. 'Peanut, that's not bad news; it's the best.'

'Hold your horses, Lieutenant. Let me finish. The thing is,' he hesitates once more, 'those Invincibles that you're up against in this morning's challenge … well, Ryker's now one of them. He's joined up with them.'

Ruby gasps.

Jack stumbles backwards, winded from the revelation.

'I accidentally found him while I was searching for Herodus' chamber. His isn't that far away from his own, and he told me.'

Jack's blood begins to boil. 'You're telling us that we're killing ourselves to get him out of here, and he's gone and become chummy with the enemy!'

'Mate, I thought that at first, too, but it's not like that. He's pretending to have changed his allegiance so he can be on the inside for Max.'

'Wow, he's a legend!' De Beer says with admiration.

But this only angers Jack more, and heightens his suspicions. Why has he gone and done something so stupid? Why didn't he just wait? He knew they were coming … Something's not right about all of this. It doesn't sit well with him. He questions Ryker's motives. Bottom line, he just doesn't trust him … again.

Peanut must've seen the murderous look in his eyes. 'Mate, are you okay?'

No, he's definitely not. How can he be?

'Listen,' Peanut continues, 'Ryker has given me the heads-up on what's gonna happen later. He's told me what the challenge is, and what you guys are to expect, but more to the point, he's given me instructions on how to fight back.'

This stops Jack dead in his tracks. His jealousy has once again clouded his reasoning, and now, weighed down with regret, he realises that he could've potentially ruined everything for them with his way of thinking. He shuts down those destructive thoughts and makes an effort to take on board what Peanut and Ryker have planned.

33

ꟼ SPY

Peanut is pumped. He's feeling pretty pleased with himself for being able to help Jack, Ruby and the others get better prepared for the inevitable battle. His gut clenches when he thinks of what they have to go through later, though. If only he could've got his hands on the gear stashed in Herodus' chamber … *I can't give up. There's gotta be a way to get in there … their lives depend upon it!*

Peanut decides to try once more. There's no way of getting in through that small barred window, so he takes a risk and enters the passageways again hoping to get in there from the inside. His heart thumps as he inches his way through the dark, abandoned corridors. The only light he has to see with comes from the small oil-fuelled wall sconces. His breathing accelerates as he gets nearer. He tries to calm himself, sure that he'll wake someone from the sound of his heavy breathing alone.

Get a grip, ya twit! You're invisible. No one can see you!

He soon comes across the door he's been looking for … or is it? A moment of indecision has him questioning if it's the right chamber. This time there's no guard securing the entry, so he's suddenly filled with uncertainty. He stands for several minutes, petrified, with his hand on the cold iron handle, doubting himself.

Okay, so if it's not the right room, I just go to the next one, right? No biggie.

He holds his breath, shuts his eyes tight and, saying a silent prayer that it's not bolted from the inside, tests the door to see if he can get in. It makes a sudden loud click, and he almost passes out from panic. And then, at practically the same moment, he hears someone approaching from up the passageway. His heart just about stops.

A guard appears, walking towards him.

Peanut throws himself up against the wall. *I'm invisible … I'm invisible … I'm invisible.*

The guard carries something, but Peanut doesn't

think to look at it until he's almost on top of him, and then the reality of what that *something* is hits him in the gut like a sledge hammer … it's Max. *Oh my God! What've they done? They've killed her!*

She's almost unrecognisable. Her hair has been cut off, and her form appears to have disintegrated to nothing. She lays limp in his arms with her head dangling lifelessly.

Just then the door beside him swings open and Herodus looks out. Peanut holds back from yelping out in surprise.

'What is the meaning of this?' Herodus says. 'How dare you try to enter my chamber?'

The guard falls back, numb at the accusation.

'She is to be taken to the next chamber, not to mine. I thought that I had made that clear.'

The guard remains speechless.

'You have disturbed my slumber. Is it your wish to lose your head over this? Now get her out of my sights! And make sure you return her to her duties before dawn, for she must resume her punishment.'

Peanut watches as the guard hastily pushes open the door next to Herodus' chamber and dumps Max onto the bed.

Thank God, at least she's alive!

Herodus stands rigid, at attention, scrutinising the task from the doorway.

Peanut notices that he's left the door to the supplies he needs wide open, but the shock of seeing Max the way she is makes him flounder. Does he dart into Herodus' room, grab one of the backpacks, then get out while he's got the chance, or does he sneak into Max's room to make sure she's okay?

His indecision costs him. The door to Max's chamber is quickly bolted shut, and Herodus returns to his bed. The guard remains sentinel over his prisoner.

Peanut stands there dumbfounded. There's nothing he can do now. He slams his hand to his mouth to hold back from cursing loudly at himself for being so stupid. He needs to get out of there, fast.

He runs, careless of the racket he's making and the attention he's drawing to his invisible self, and he doesn't stop until he's made it out to the arena. Once there, he finds a place to hide. Deep within the stadium ruins and new construction, he buries himself and waits.

34

ᴇTERNAL ᴇREST

Peanut wakes in a panic from his doze, sees he's no longer invisible and immediately phases again. Dawn is just breaking, and the workers have returned to the construction site, ready for another day of labouring. They know, too well, that they need to have the arena ready for today's challenge.

Peanut needs to make a move before he's found out. He looks towards the drawbridge, his only way of escape, but it's still up. *What the hell? Now what?* If the workers haven't entered via the drawbridge, where have they come from? Desperate for another way out, Peanut scans the arena and sees a steady flow of them coming from the depths of the passageways beneath the arena. Clearly, there's another way to get in, and he figures that if there's a way in, then there must be a way out.

Not having time to lose, he runs back through the corridors, bumping into the stream of workers coming towards him, oblivious of the commotion he's making. Finally, he makes his way to an unfamiliar exit. It's still mostly dark outside, but he realises he's stumbled into a market place. It's too early for any bustling activity, but a few village people are already up and preparing their wares and foodstuff for the new day.

He needs to find his way back to the others and warn them about the battle later today, and he can't waste another second. But which way does he go? He runs through the market area looking for a way back to the forest, but every turn he takes leads him to a dead end. An endless line of attached stone buildings forms a barrier just as formidable as the fortress walls. There's no escape. If only he could get to the other side of these buildings, there might be some hope.

And that's when he sees it. A door to one of the homes opens as one of the villagers prepares to exit. Peanut dives on top of him, pushing him to the ground, and then clambers over him to enter the building. He hastily looks for a back exit. From one of the barred windows, he can see the forest within reach. Now in a panic, he runs through the corridors of the home looking for a way to get out there, and finally he comes across a locked iron gate that leads to the outside. He throws himself against it, trying to loosen it from its hinges by repeatedly ramming it with his body weight until he feels it budge.

He's oblivious to the owner of the home—the one he knocked down earlier. The man stands to one side guarding his family from the inexplicable phenomenon occurring before them. Completely confounded, he watches the heavy iron gate fall to the ground, seemingly of its own accord.

Peanut finally makes his escape. He can now see enough in the darkness to get about, and prays that he can find his way back to the others. But he needs to hurry … there's not much time. It's up to him to prevent this battle from happening. He's got a fair idea of the direction in which he should be heading, so he takes off without a minute to spare.

After a while, however, although initially confident, he realises he's nowhere near where he's supposed to be. He starts to worry. The terrain of the forest is still unfamiliar to him, and by now it shouldn't be. But he continues, carefully descending a steep slope. The filtered light coming through the forest canopy grows dimmer until he's almost in complete darkness again. *This can't be right. Man, how did I get so lost?*

And it's not so much that he doesn't remember the forest being like this that makes him realise his mistake, it's the sudden eeriness that grips him. It just feels wrong. 'Geez, has it just dropped twenty degrees, or what?' He rubs his arms to stir up some heat.

Something unseen suddenly rushes past him. The surprise makes him stumble backwards and fall flat on his butt. He scrambles to get back up and prepare himself for it to return. His gaze darts in every direction, and his heart skips a beat not knowing what's coming. And there is something out there. He can feel it. Whatever it is, he has no idea, but the one thing that he's sure of is that it doesn't seem natural. Deep down, his senses are telling him to get the hell out of there.

He clambers up the slope as if he's escaping Hell itself and runs as far away from the place as possible. He doesn't even stop to look back. In his rush to get away, he doesn't hear something coming towards him until he slams head on with Medwin, propelling the small man into the scrub from the impact.

'Medwin! Man, I'm sorry about that. Hey, are you okay?'

Medwin gets himself up and brushes the leaves and twigs from the sack he's wearing. 'By *okay* do you mean to ask if I am injured? Because I am well. Do not trouble yourself, young Peanut.'

'Man, I'm stoked that I've run into you. I know where Jack and Ruby are, and I've just come back from seeing Ryker and Max. I need to get to the squad before the battle begins.'

'Then follow me. I fear that we have little time.'

As he follows his new friend, Peanut explains what's happened.

'And where were you running from just now?' Medwin asks. 'The terror in your eyes was unmistakable. 'Twas as though you chanced upon a spirit. Did you happen to venture into the Valley of Lost Souls?'

'The Valley of what?'

''Tis a place where our spirit goes for eternal rest.'

'You mean, dead people! Is that what that was? Man, that place gave me the creeps.'

'You would do well to stay away from there, my friend.'

'Hey, no worries about that. There's no way in Hell I'll be going back there any time soon.'

Medwin chuckles. 'I am struggling to make sense of your words, but it amuses me that I am somehow able to understand you. Come, make haste. For I sense that your news will be very much welcomed.'

35

Where's The Cavalry?

Ryker

The time has come. The battle is here. Ryker has done all he can to assure the realm champions where his allegiance lies. Archimedes was his toughest judge. Ryker eventually put the man's well-placed suspicions to rest after his award-winning performance. Ryker secretly smiles, congratulating himself on how convincing he was. He told them lies and stroked their egos, and did everything in his power to leave them without a doubt that he'd switched camp and was eager to fight for them and annihilate the opposition. He was so persuasive that at one stage he even had himself convinced of his own stories. And now, due to his efforts, they're totally 'Team Ryker.'

The crowd roar as he enters the arena with the four Invincibles. For the first time, the spectators see the champions in a formation without their beloved Beowulf. And from their excitement, it's clear that they don't disapprove of his replacement. Their morbid curiosity makes them keen to see what the new champion has to offer in way of entertainment.

And for their added pleasure, Herodus is a little more dramatic in their presentation today. The fabulous five rise like Gods to the stage on a platform secreted below the ground of the arena—something straight out of a gladiator movie. And Ryker knows that, just like in those movies, they're going to be battling the same.

He glances across and makes eye contact with Jack, but to his alarm, Jack looks murderous. Something's not right. Confused, but determined, he lets him know by a subtle nod of the head that they're on the same team. To his relief, Jack discreetly returns the gesture.

Okay, so it's all just an act.

He looks at the others. Ruby, of course, will be okay with her legendary shield, so this calms him a little. And seeing the two task-force members makes him feel more confident for them. These guys are huge and definitely a force to be reckoned with.

Herodus runs through his spiel before calling on their Noble Ruler to make his address and later officiate at the obligatory sacrificial ceremony.

Ryker welcomes this interval and hopes that they take their time, because he knows the battle will begin directly following these formalities … and any delay in getting started can only be a good thing.

He scans the arena looking for any tell-tale signs of the intervention. He prays that Peanut and the rescue team are already here, waiting in the fringes. There's no way he's going into battle. He could never intentionally hurt any of his friends. *But did Peanut have enough time to get back to them?*

His thoughts become scrambled, and he hears Archimedes' voice in his head: *Remember, they are your adversaries, and you will annihilate them! They have triumphed in the past and have rejoiced in it. They have used you ill, and have returned only to torment and make a mockery of you.*

Ryker feels his words starting to penetrate to a deeper level. The old, deranged Ryker begins to resurface, and for a moment he allows it. He needs to act and look the part of a realm champion. He lets it stir up his aggression, but at the same time he holds onto the reins of control with an iron-fisted grip.

He won't let him dominate. Archimedes will not be turning him against his friends.

Ryker paces back and forth with a determined look of bubbling hostility, and when he's convinced that Archimedes has bought the act, he shuts him down. He then throws in a few loud, intimidating growls and curses for added measure.

Athos has been watching him with concern. 'Ryker, I approve of your fervour, but you must show some restraint. At this pace you will peak too soon.'

But Shant appears to be more than ready to get this battle started. 'Nonsense, he is young and resilient. I applaud his zeal. I, too, say that we attack now, while they least expect it, before the ritual ends.'

Ryker secretly laughs at his ability to manipulate them so easily.

Vyvian eyes him with unmistakable admiration. He smiles a crooked smile, then gives her a cheeky wink. *There, that should throw her off her game.* And like a charm, her cheeks flush with heat.

The ceremony finishes and Pius makes his final address. Ryker's chest is about to burst from uneasiness. He concentrates on singing his favourite song, and this brings him a little calm.

'… and let the battle begin!'

What! Already? But where's Peanut?

Ryker can't breathe. There's no intervention, no

reinforcement, no nothing. It's come down to this … he has no choice; he must go into battle.

A tortured cry of pain from the other side snaps him to attention. One of the soldiers is on the ground in a foetal position, holding his head like it's going to explode.

The crowd cheers.

Ryker turns to see who's doing this, and realises it's the work of Archimedes. It would appear that he's further developed his mind-control powers such that he can now inflict debilitating pain. How had he not realised earlier that this was possible? He looks back at Archimedes' victim who's squirming in agony on the ground. *Block him out!*

Jack yells the same warning, 'De Beer, don't let him in. Remember, you need to block him.'

Ryker watches as De Beer gradually stops writhing. But no sooner does he stop when the second soldier falls to the ground in the same tortured pain. Archimedes is clearly revelling in his newfound power.

Jack's anger is obvious. He turns into a raging bull and charges Archimedes, knocking him to the ground and breaking his mental hold. He delivers punches in a ruthless onslaught, pounding him until his fists are bloodied. Archimedes struggles to fight back.

The crowd cheers, loving the comeback.

The second soldier, now recovered from Archimedes' attack, pulls out a switchblade concealed in his boot and dives onto Athos, delivering blow after blow of potentially fatal strikes.

The crowd gasps as one.

The soldier stumbles back, his breathing heavy, shocked to see the old man unaffected. The gaping wounds to his chest miraculously heal over.

The audience cheers.

'Gallo, he's indestructible. You can't kill him,' Jack yells out to him.

Athos takes advantage of the soldier's moment of disbelief and returns the attack. Though momentarily dumbfounded by the old man's strength, Gallo quickly retaliates. They battle one on one.

Ryker needs to make a move if they're going to believe he's changed allegiance. He looks around to see what action to take and makes a beeline for De Beer. He bowls him over, dives on top of him, grabs him in a choke-hold, and then pretends to pound his face with several powerful undercuts.

'We just need some more time. The taskforce should be here any minute,' De Beer tells him through clenched teeth as he puts on a good performance in retaliating. He throws Ryker over his shoulder, then knocks him to the ground. They wrestle convincingly, kicking up dust to mask their acting.

A sudden wind shift alerts Ryker that Shant is about to cause havoc. 'He's conjuring up a tornado,' he informs De Beer. 'Stay close to Ruby, she'll protect you.' He then shoves him in her direction in time for Ruby to shelter them all within her dome.

'Vyvian, prepare yourself,' Shant calls out the order just as he vacuums all four of them into his twisting funnel.

Ryker watches in horror as Vyvian flies into the sky and readies her arrows.

This could be the end of them. He needs to do something, but what? He can't do anything without giving himself away. He watches on helplessly as his friends tumble uncontrollably within the tornado. Ruby's shield now only protects her.

Once again, the spectators become boisterous with approval.

But before Vyvian has time to draw her first arrow, the tornado implodes. Ruby encases them in her transparent barrier once again and returns them safely to the ground.

The Invincibles look at each other, infuriated. 'We need to take out the red-head. Ryker, you are the only one that can do that.'

He looks at Archimedes incredulously. 'And how do you expect me to do that? You've seen her shield;

it's impenetrable.'

'Use your strength to raise the dome and shake them until they are divided and without her protection again, just as Shant had succeeded in doing earlier. But this time, we will be ready. The very moment that you have achieved this, we will act. Invincibles be prepared. There are four of them to our five. Vyvian, you are to take out the girl. Athos, you will act on the warrior you battled earlier. Shant you will deal with the other, and I will take on the boy. Enough said, let us advance.'

Ryker's gut clenches. Archimedes' plan might just work, and now he's got no choice but to do it. His heart starts pounding, and his breathing accelerates. He wipes away the sweat from his brow and prepares to put on a convincing performance. He lets out a tremendous roar of frustration, but to all others it sounds like a battle cry.

The crowd starts chanting, 'Ryker, Ryker, Ryker …'

He turns to look at the eager expression on the faces of his true enemies, and swallows the bile that's risen to his mouth. His hand has been forced. He has no choice. He makes his move, and as he reluctantly approaches his friends, he prays that Peanut turns up in time to pull a rabbit out of a hat.

But then the situation takes a rapid nosedive. He

hears a sound that fills him with dread, something he knew was coming, but had no power to prevent. Lions. The wild beasts surface, roaring, from the dungeons beneath the arena floor.

The crowd gasps in surprise.

In moments, several lions fill the stadium. Ryker's heart stutters. Flashbacks of Jaeger's tragic death come back to haunt him. In his tormented, delusional mind, he was hoping that the plans to use them had been overlooked.

'Act swiftly, Ryker!' Archimedes calls out. 'For the animals will impede our success.'

Ryker looks at the alarmed faces of his friends as he stands before them ready to take hold of the shield.

'What are you doing!' Ruby asks, panic in her voice.

'Believe me, if I could prevent this from happening, I would. Be ready, as soon as I've broken down your control, Ruby, they're going to strike. They're gunning for you. You need to just protect yourself. The others might be able to stave off the attack.'

'What? No!'

But Ryker has run out of options. Vyvian hovers nearby, ready. He squats before them and grabs hold of the shield. Then with an enormous effort he raises all four of them off the ground ready to shake them from their safety.

Gallo cries out for him to stop. 'Ryker, just let Ruby cover you too. Together we'll figure a way out of here. They won't be able to touch us.'

'He's right,' De Beer pleads. 'Listen to him. Without Ruby we don't stand a chance. We've got no weapons. Those lions will kill us!'

As he struggles to secure a firm foothold to carry out the deed, a piece of Ryker dies inside him. He struggles to hold back his tears. And then he dares to look Jack in the eye. 'I can't … I've got no choice … they'll kill Max.'

He can't bear to look at their desperate faces as they topple over each other the moment he starts to shake the sphere. Behind him he hears the excited encouragement from the enemy and the crowd. His self-loathing only intensifies. And as expected, Ruby's ability to protect her friends disintegrates. The resistance of the shield now protects only her.

Vyvian isn't quick enough to take out Ruby, so she turns her focus on one of the soldiers … Gallo. She fires her arrow. Instinctively he throws an arm up to protect himself, and to all their amazement, he somehow deflects it without even touching it. Vyvian shoots another, and just as before, the arrow ricochets off.

As she readies herself to repeat the attack, Jack yells at him to try repelling her. 'Channel that force you're feeling and drive her back.'

Gallo, quick to understand, casts his hands in her direction in a fending-off motion. And to their astonishment, an invisible force flings Vyvian metres away.

Ryker is gobsmacked and ecstatic at the same time, but because of this surprising development, he hasn't been conscious of the predatory movement of the animals around them. It's only when he hears De Beer's cries of pain that he realises what's happened. One of the lions has taken him down and he's fighting for his life.

Gallo uses his newfound power to throw off De Beer's attacker, but the beast has tasted blood and races back for more.

The audience cheers and stamp their feet.

Ryker is helpless to do anything. He looks around anxiously and realises that even if there was a way to rescue him, he couldn't because, right now, a lion is stalking him. He braces himself for the attack, but strangely, the animal suddenly falls to the ground thrashing about in obvious pain. Archimedes has come to his aid. Ryker acknowledges this with an appreciative nod.

The crowd gasps.

Ryker turns, and his eyes widen at what he witnesses, something beyond anything he's ever seen or even imagined. De Beer's body transforms, morphing into an armour-covered, impenetrable entity. Reflective, metallic, fish-like scales protect his whole body—his very own personal shield.

Gallo once again repels the lion before helping De Beer to his feet, and Ruby is quick to secure both soldiers and Jack within her dome once again. All four stand united, now, more than ever, ready for anything the Invincibles may have up their sleeves.

Ryker's relief is short-lived. He suddenly becomes aware of the animals circling the Invincibles, once again hungry to attack.

Athos calls out for Shant to conjure up a tornado. Vyvian readies herself, waiting until the animals are whipped into the whirling funnel of air before launching her strike. One by one the arrows hit their mark, and very soon the threat has passed.

Ryker checks to make sure his friends are still safe. When he sees they are, he lowers his face to mask his relief.

'Do not fret, young Ryker,' Archimedes says, misunderstanding his reaction. 'We will reform and destroy them. As before, we need to divide them to defeat them. If we repeat our attack on the shield and then act quickly, then we will have our victory.

Vyvian, your earlier hesitation cost us. You must remain vigilant. You have two targets now: the girl and the serpent warrior. You must first take out the girl. Without her, the others remain vulnerable.'

'And what do you suggest I do with the serpent warrior? You, yourself, witnessed his impenetrable armour.'

'Fire your arrow into one of his eyes,' Shant instructs. 'He has little protection there, and a direct hit will finish him.'

Ryker bites back from reacting to their callousness. Instead, he walks away and paces back and forth, trying to contain his sudden rage.

Archimedes stops him and places his hand on his arm. 'Ryker, you must prepare yourself. Your revenge is near. Do not allow them to make a mockery of you. Contain your frustration and channel it to overthrow them, for it will all come to naught if you do not succeed. If by chance the opportunity arises that you yourself can take out the girl, then do it. The glory will be yours, and yours alone. You will be hailed a hero.' Archimedes stares Ryker in the eye, almost salivating with the taste of victory so close.

Ryker struggles to keep up the façade. His stomach churns, and he almost chokes on the bile that gurgles up to his mouth again. He can't do this. He can't kill his friends. But if he doesn't, Herodus will kill Max. He throws off Archimedes' hold on him and begins to pace again. His head throbs from his indecision, but to all others watching, it would appear that he's preparing himself for the attack.

The others stand ready, waiting for his sign to go forth.

But before they get a chance to make their move, a blast shakes the foundation of the arena, alerting them to a different type of attack. From behind the cloud of dust, he sees a big gaping hole where the fortress wall once was.

The crowd scream and, hysterical with fear, try to evacuate all at once, creating sudden pandemonium.

Ryker almost collapses with relief. He can finally breathe easy.

36

LOGAN STRIKES

PEANUT

Peanut's detour to the Valley of Lost Souls cost the taskforce precious time—time they didn't have. Now, as they plough through the forest to rescue his friends, his mind races as to what might be happening in the arena. He has no idea when they'd scheduled the challenge and is almost jumping out of his skin with worry that they might be too late. Jack, Ruby and the others will have little to no chance in this battle without the help of the unit. When Ryker told him about the lions, his heart had just about stopped. He hopes Ruby is able to hold it together long enough to keep them safe until they arrive.

As they approach the arena, they can hear the

spectators suddenly become highly excited. Peanut's gut clenches. He turns to Kenny and sees panic in his expression too. They've already begun.

Captain Logan immediately goes into tactical mode, ordering his two men, Callaghan and Goosen, to set up the detonators as per the plan. Peanut and Kenny lie low, waiting for instruction. They'd left the doctor and the vice admiral behind in lockdown at the tree-house. Logan insisted that they remain there since their presence could potentially jeopardise the whole operation.

Suddenly the crowd cries out in alarm. Peanut is beside himself. The unknown of what's happening in there is killing him. Kenny reaches out to stop Peanut from making any rash moves.

'But what's taking them so long?' Peanut grits through clenched teeth.

And then he sees the two soldiers returning from their task. They're carefully retracing their steps, unreeling the roll of conductive wire that's crucial for this to work. Once they're in position, Logan signals for the detonators to be triggered. A loud explosion follows.

Peanut and Kenny duck for cover as debris from the blast showers them. The sound of complete mayhem follows: screams from within the arena as spectators scramble to get away. Peanut chances a look and sees a huge hole in the side wall of the fortress. At the entrance, hundreds of people flee by means of the lowered bridge. He waits anxiously, hoping to spot his friends amongst them.

Movement grabs his attention at the site of the explosion. He watches in disbelief as a dusty figure appears out of the ruins. If he's not mistaken, it's De Beer. And three others follow close behind. Peanut's heart rate accelerates when he recognises Ruby and Jack. They dart into the forest to get away.

Moments later, Kenny nudges Peanut and points up to the sky. Peanut spots Vyvian on the lookout, hovering up high. He starts to panic. She'll easily spot them and foil their escape. Peanut wants to yell out a warning for them to stop running and just lie low. There's a good chance she won't see them if they remain still. He stands from his crouched position, ready to call out, but Kenny dives on him, clearly having anticipated his reaction, and quietly blasts him.

Peanut catches a threatening look from Logan too, warning him to stay down and to not do anything stupid.

But Peanut can't do that—it's not in his DNA. He needs to do something—but what? Suddenly a thought comes to him, and then, defying Logan's unspoken command, he vanishes and takes off in the opposite direction. Once he's at a safe distance from the others, he materialises and, in typical Peanut style, makes as much of a ruckus as he can muster to create a distraction. He whips at the bushes and trips clumsily over the roots trying to catch Vyvian's attention. He turns to see whether she's spotted him, and to his relief, she has. Grinning with excitement, she spins around to tell the others.

Behind him he hears the thrashing sound of a chase and assumes that the rest of the Invincibles are now on his tail, but he doesn't stop. Once he's confident that he's totally diverted their attention from the others, he vanishes—thankfully just in the nick of time, because Vyvian was close to being on top of him, and he can hear the rest of them fast approaching.

Peanut dives behind a large boulder and tries to slow his erratic breathing. He's sweating bullets and needs to settle himself right down if he's not to get caught.

Vyvian, now directly above him, calls to the others that she's lost her target. She hovers there, waiting for the others to catch up.

'Vyvian, fly higher for a better vantage,' Athos tells her, sounding as if he's stopped a moment to catch his breath. 'Shant, Archimedes, Ryker, we must disperse. One in each direction. Keep your senses alert; they cannot have gone far. Now, go.'

Peanut watches as they all dart into the forest. Ryker holds back for a moment, enough time for Peanut to whisper. 'What the hell are you doing? Get out of here!'

'Peanut!'

'Now's your chance. I'll meet you back at the tree-house.'

Just then, Vyvian circles back. 'Ryker, did something catch your eye?'

'I thought I had, but I was wrong. What can you see?'

'Nothing, they must have secreted themselves. But you are wise to stop and take in the sounds, for they will expose themselves soon enough. They cannot hide forever. I will tell the others to do the same.' And then she's off.

'Peanut, you need to go before she gets to them. As soon as they stop running, they'll hear you,' Ryker warns him.

'What about you?'

Ryker hesitates a moment, clearly at odds over something, then tells Peanut that he'll be right behind him.

While Peanut has the chance to go, he does. He just hopes Ryker doesn't take too long to make his move.

37

BACK AT THE TREE-HOUSE

JACK

Jack can't believe it; they're finally out. They make a bee-line for the forest, hoping to use the web of the undergrowth to escape detection. He spots Vyvian hovering above the drawbridge, clearly determined to hunt them down, and he calls out a warning to De Beer for them to stop and hide. They dive for cover.

From his refuge, he watches her movements. Something catches her attention, and she's quick to act on it, darting in the opposite direction. Jack hopes she hasn't spotted his friends. He squats down low and listens, figuring that the Invincibles will quickly act on her sighting, and, sure enough, they do. Jack hears them chasing someone through the undergrowth.

Gallo stands and motions for them to follow him, and they move further into the woods. A short while later, De Beer, trailing at the rear, lets out a short inconspicuous whistle. Gallo signals for them to drop and fall silent. Jack grabs Ruby's hand and pulls her down with him. They squat beneath a fern, listening. His heart pumps furiously, preparing him to act at a moment's notice.

An identical whistle comes from the depths of the woods. Jack relaxes instantly, and Ruby breathes out a sigh of relief. Gallo returns the signal, and, within seconds, Logan appears with Kenny, Goosen and Callaghan.

But where's Peanut?

Logan stops Jack reacting by assuring him that Peanut shouldn't be too far behind them. 'He saved your necks, the impulsive idiot. He used himself as a decoy to distract Vyvian from spotting you.'

'Oh, no! Poor Peanut,' Ruby cries out.

'Poor Peanut! He's bloody lucky it worked. Knee-jerk reactions like that will jeopardise this operation,' Logan spits out.

'Yeah, but like you said, it worked didn't it?' Jack retorts. Even though he'll defend Peanut to the death each and every time, he secretly curses the dumb-ass for being so reckless. 'What you don't get,' Jack adds in frustration, 'is that we know how these guys think and how they work. In fact, we know a whole heap of stuff, so maybe you should be listening to us. Ask us what we think. Keep us in the loop.'

'You're here, aren't you?' Logan strikes back. 'Look, if we had any concerns, we would've got you kids involved, but we didn't, okay? We had it all planned out and under control.'

'Plans? Like what? I bet Kenny didn't know about these plans.' He looks at Kenny and immediately knows he's right.

'We had a strategy. We would've firstly held them off with some of the tactical gear we've brought, like the tear-gas grenades—'

'Yeah, but for how long?' Kenny interrupts, his tone just as annoyed. 'Peanut diverted the enemy away from us, got them off our tail. That's got to be a good thing, right?'

Great point, Kenny!

'Sure, if what he's done has really worked. I hate to point out the obvious, but where is he?'

'I wouldn't give up on him just yet,' Ruby says. 'He'll turn up like a bad penny. You'll see.'

'That might be so, but I'd hate to end up risking the lives of my men to find him if he doesn't.'

Logan is right; the situation isn't great, and Jack knows it. They had two of his friends to worry about, and now they've got three. He needs to back off a little. They can't be at each other's throats. He takes a moment to calm the situation, and soon they're following the marked clues they'd left earlier back to the tree-house, all with a better attitude.

As they silently make their way, Jack's thoughts return to Peanut. What if he's lost out there somewhere, or worse still, what if he's been caught? But before he starts to panic, Medwin steps out of the bush in front of them.

'Young Jack, I had a vision that our paths would cross today,' he says.

'Medwin, do you know what's happened to Peanut? He took off into the forest, and I'm worried that he's been caught.'

'Do not fret; I will go in search of him. I sense he is not in any danger … at least at present he is not.'

'So you're able to look into the future, are you?' Logan asks Medwin with interest. 'That's amazing. Maybe you can predict what's going to happen here.'

'This I cannot tell you with confidence. Only time will tell, I'm afraid. And as for our friend, Peanut, I must set out at once. There is an unmistakable need to guide him straight. This vision I have of him is more accurately defined.'

Logan snorts. 'Yeah, this I can readily believe.'

Soon after, they join the rest of the team at the treehouse, and Logan shares what he learned about Medwin's super power, his curiosity clearly piqued by his interaction with the small man. When Ruby reveals what happened in the arena with Gallo and De Beer, his eyes light up. 'You mean to say that we've all got the potential to transform? That's incredible!'

Jack reminds him that the super-power you take on is more than likely going to be your own natural ability, only amplified. 'So you see, both Gallo and De Beer transformed into these cool beings that are purely an exaggeration of their own ability to defend.'

'You think it'd happen to me, too?'

'I guess we're all capable of some kind of transformation,' Kenny tells him. 'Has anything heightened with you since we've been here?'

'Well, you could say that my thought processes are much more in tune. I'm thinking with better clarity than I ever have.'

'It makes sense, you being in command and all,' Ruby says. 'It's a bit like Kenny. His brain is like it's on steroids when he needs to think of things.'

'Wow! I just put it down to the adrenalin rush I was getting from being here.'

'And I'd put money on it that Professor Rutherford has got the power to heal, just like Max has,' Kenny adds. 'And I imagine, sir,' Kenny gulps nervously as he turns to the vice admiral, 'only because we've seen how strong Ryker is, that you'll probably have the same super-power as him.'

Ryker's dad gets up, calmly walks up to a massive tree and wraps his arms around its huge trunk, then casually yanks it out of the ground as if it was no effort at all. The birds resting in it take flight at the invasion.

Everyone stands back, looking apprehensive, not knowing what he's planning to do with it now he's pulled it out. The vice admiral's eyes sparkle and his lips curl upwards, almost laughing, at his predicament.

'You'll find that everyone, to a degree, has a super-power here,' Kenny tells them. 'Some more obvious than others. Medwin has intuition, and the guards, although some of them are as dumb as a box of rocks, are built like tanks, and super strong. Herodus on the other hand, although being just as strong, is a whole heap smarter, and very much like you, Captain Logan, a sharp thinker.'

'What about us?' Goosen asks for Callaghan and himself.

'Well, what are you good at?' Kenny asks.

Goosen explains that he was a track runner before joining the forces, and Callaghan qualified for the Olympic swim team when he was younger. After a few experimental exercises, they find that Goosen could rival Edra with his speed, and Callaghan can hold his breath for twenty minutes without passing out.

So, between the lot of them, Jack figures they've got a pretty good chance of getting out of here alive.

But first, they just need to find Peanut.

38

WHAT'S HIS GAME?

JACK

Later, to Jack's relief, Medwin returns with their impulsive friend. And just as he'd predicted, the twit had got himself lost.

Peanut tells them all about his encounter with Ryker. 'He's planning on giving the Invincibles the slip,' he finishes. 'So we should expect him soon.'

'I cannot see that come to being,' Medwin says.

'Why? What have you seen in your vision?' the vice admiral asks, suddenly anxious for his son.

''Tis not my vision, but my understanding of Ryker's mind that indicates this to me.'

This surprises everyone but Jack. The look in Ryker's eyes just before he shook them out of the protection of Ruby's shield, and his vow to look out for Max, made it clear that he wasn't coming back to them any time soon. Jack's stomach churns with a roller-coaster ride of emotions. The guy's either a legend, or he's someone Jack should feel threatened by. Is there something behind his motives that go beyond gratitude and obligation?

Jack tries to get his head around it. He might be too late. This thing he thought he had with Max may never happen now. He's in a world of torment not knowing: not knowing what Ryker's motives are; not knowing if they'll ever get out of here; not knowing if Max is okay. All he knows is what Medwin told them earlier, that she's being used to heal the injured. But what does that mean?

'Peanut, did Ryker tell you anything more about Max?' Jack asks later when they're alone. 'Has he been able to be there for her?'

Peanut stiffens.

'What! You know something, don't you?'

But Peanut clams up.

This is so unlike him that it has Jack's heart racing. 'Mate, what is it?'

'Nothing. Geez, will ya quit it! It's like Medwin told us, she's helping with the medical stuff.'

But Jack isn't buying it. He glares at his friend until Peanut relents.

'Okay, look,' he says with a sigh. 'I didn't mention it before because I didn't want you or her dad worrying, but I saw her. She was asleep, mind you,' he adds quickly, 'so I didn't get a chance to talk to her or anything, okay? And I couldn't wake her without giving myself away, all right?'

Jack can't understand his over-the-top defensiveness. Something's not right. 'So what makes you think I'd start worrying just because you saw her sleeping?'

'Maybe that was the wrong choice of words. I know how cut up you are about the mess she's in, so maybe I just chose not to say anything, that's all. Okay?'

Jack knows that he's hiding something. He can feel it, but he doesn't push further. 'How did she look?'

'Peaceful … she was asleep, right?'

Jack looks at him from the corner of his eye and says nothing.

'What about that Ryker, huh? I just don't get it,' Peanut says, shifting the focus of the conversation. 'He told me he was gonna be right behind me. What's he playing at? You know something, I reckon all this power's gone straight to his head. If ya ask me, he's gone nuts again. Well, if he wants to change horses in midstream, I say let him. I'm done with all of his crap, and so should you. As soon as we've got Max, I'm out of here.'

'Come on, Peanut, I don't think it's anything like that.'

'No? Well, how come when he had the chance to get away, he didn't, huh? You told me De Beer gave him a get-out-of-gaol card during the battle; and I know he had the perfect opportunity to take off while he was out in the open, but he didn't take either one.'

For no logical reason, Jack's world tilts on its axis again. Peanut's doubt has made him question everything. Could Ryker have a hidden agenda? He shakes those demons from his head, knowing that what he saw in Ryker's eyes earlier was real. *You can't fake stuff like that! But why, then, does he feel the need to be Max's hero? Why doesn't he just leave it for the taskforce to get her out of there?*

He turns away from Peanut and pulls at his hair, inwardly screaming in frustration. He decides that he needs to stop reacting like a cave-man and start trusting what he saw. 'Peanut, enough, man! Quit with your hunches, will ya? You weren't there when he said he needed to stay back for Max, okay? He meant it!'

'Hey, keep your shirt on! You're probably right. I'm no expert, you know. I was just saying.'

And it's that relaxed, off-hand way of thinking that makes Jack want to knock his best friend's block off.

39

Delirium

Max

Max feels safe and warm. And for the first time in a long time, she's in a happy place ... she's with her Mum. She curls herself up into a ball next to her, savouring the moment, but in no time she feels her rise to leave. Max looks up and returns her mother's smile as she waves goodbye.

But then everything changes ... something's wrong. Her mother's eyes go wide, and Max sees instant terror there. And then she's gone ... vanished into nothingness.

Suddenly, her mother's hands reach out of the surrounding abyss, clawing in a desperate attempt to grab hold of something—anything. Her face appears as if in a mist, mouth opening and closing without sound, her eyes begging to be saved.

Max needs to get to her. Now!

But try as she may, she can't make her legs move. She's entangled, ensnared by an invisible trap.

Her vision blurs, and her mother's features start to fade. Max rubs at her eyes. It doesn't look like her now. Was she wrong? Is it even her? But now's not the time to think. She's losing her. She's running out of time. With all that she has, Max struggles against the unseen restraints tugging at her legs.

Finally, she's free.

But now she's somehow waist deep in a sea of red, and it's rising at a rate that's threatening to drown her. *Where has this come from?* With desperate urgency she clambers through the thick, red fluid, trying to reach her beloved mother.

And then she sees her father, and he's just standing there … watching. She tries to scream for help, but no sound comes out. Her voice remains unheard. All of a sudden, he turns and calmly walks away.

She loses her footing and is dragged under. Down, down, deeper she goes. In her desperation to fill her screaming lungs with air, she gulps mouthfuls of the thick, metallic-tasting fluid.

She's weakening. She prays for more strength. The muscles in her legs burn, but she can't give up now. She sees her mother bobbing lifelessly in the murky waters. It's up to her to save her. There's no one else.

She's so close, but she needs to dig deeper still … and she somehow does. From a strength within, she finds it, and at last, she manages to inch a little closer. For a moment their fingertips touch, but she can't quite get a firm hold. She's slipping away … Max is losing her again.

No, no. NO!

Helpless to do anything, she watches in horror as her mother is sucked into a deep hollow vortex. She disappears into the sea of red, gone forever.

'Get up!'

Max is yanked from her bed. She stumbles and struggles to remain upright. Cold liquid splashes into her face. She gasps at the shock of it, and suddenly she's desperate for air. She won't let herself be drowned by the blood.

'Eshmun is waiting!'

Her head is in a thick fog. She reaches out, trying to find her mother in all of this confusion. *Mum. Mum!* A slap across the face makes her world spin. She presses her hand to her burning cheek.

'Move it!'

A solid figure before her drags her, like a garbage bag full of rubbish, through a stone passageway to a place that suddenly registers as having some meaning. She remembers now where she is and what she's doing. And just in time, because by the look on Eshmun's face, he's been waiting long enough.

'Now heal!' Herodus growls.

40

THE WORK OF THE DEVIL

RYKER

Ryker has just returned from the forest after having successfully convinced the Invincibles of his allegiance once again. He'd played the part fully by hunting for the escapees and insisting that they keep looking for them, even though, after a fruitless hour of searching, Athos was ready to count their losses.

On their way back to their chambers, Aelianna walks past them carrying a food basket. One of Herodus' guards accompanies her.

Their eyes meet fleetingly. The encounter is so

unexpected that he nearly doesn't register that it's her. He does a double-take to make sure that he's seeing right, but she passes and continues on her way without giving him a second look.

Later, as he lays on his bed thinking of her—his co-conspirator—he stops, suddenly alarmed. He realises that there was something in that brief glance they shared earlier. It's so startling that it has the hair on the back of his neck stand on end. He jolts upright.

She intended for him to know something; there was a hidden meaning in the way she looked at him. But what that message is, he can't quite grasp. His heart starts to pound. Something's gone wrong … very wrong.

'Find Eshmun, immediately!' Herodus yells from one of the chambers down the corridor.

Ryker jumps to his feet.

'The healer cannot be stirred,' Herodus continues in the same anxious voice.

Ryker looks out his door and sees Aelianna run from the same room.

'No, Aelianna, not you,' Herodus cries. 'You are to remain with her. I will send a guard. Guard!'

Ryker arrives at the chamber entrance in a heartbeat. He pushes past Herodus to get to Max. He hardly recognises her. Her wasted body lies lifeless on the ground. He falls to his knees and shakes her, desperately trying to wake her. 'Max, Max!' He turns to Aelianna, who stands at the doorway looking terrified. 'Bring me some water, quickly.'

She enters the room hesitantly, staying as far away from him as she can, and grabs a jug of water and a cloth. Then she runs to him and virtually throws them to him before scurrying for the exit where she remains outside the door watching with wide eyes.

Ryker sponges her scorching-hot face and neck. 'What have you done to her?' he accuses Herodus. 'She's burning up with a fever.'

'Burning!' Aelianna yelps as if being singed herself. She steps back a little further, clearly petrified.

Ryker continues to bath Max's skin with the cool water, praying it's enough. He's at a loss to know what else to do.

Eshmun finally arrives. He touches her skin, then jerks his hand back as if being scalded and hastily withdraws, staring at Max with terror in his eyes. Aelianna and Herodus trip over each other in an effort to move further away.

Ryker can't understand their overreaction. *It's as if they're terrified of catching Max's fever.*

'The witch has been damned!' Eshmun cries out. 'This is the work of the devil. Her skin burns like the gates of hell. She is being punished for all that is evil within her.'

Say what!

Herodus steps further back and pulls Aelianna in front of him as a shield.

'She is too far consumed to see another day,' Eshmun tells them. 'Dispose of her before we all become contaminated for her sins.'

Aelianna gasps.

'Do not just stand there,' Herodus yells at the guards. 'Take her from here. Get rid of her! Throw her into the woods, and let the wolves have her.'

Ryker sees the perfect opportunity for an escape. He gently picks up her limp body and turns to look Aelianna in the eye, hoping he can convey to her a message he doesn't dare speak. At first, Aelianna hesitates, looking a little doubtful, but then he sees understanding dawn in her eyes.

Ryker goes to leave, but Herodus stops him. 'Artemius and Dareios will take her. You will return to your chamber.'

Ryker hesitates, trying to plan his next move, but the guards are waiting, and so is Herodus. Realising that he's powerless to do anything, he lays her back down and steps away. Max is getting out, and that's all he needs to focus on at the moment.

He watches helplessly as the two guards take her unconscious body. He can only pray that they don't just dump her, as Herodus has ordered, for the wild animals to devour.

'Aelianna, you, too, must leave,' Herodus tells her as he steps away from her in haste. 'Go. Cleanse yourself of the filth that has tainted your skin. For it is a certainty that you, too, have been infected.'

Aelianna nods and leaves. Herodus and Eshmun scurry away in a panic.

Ryker prays that Aelianna has faith enough in him to go against her superstitious fears and do everything she can to protect Max. Now with Max safe, he only has himself to fend for. And that, he knows, will be a walk in the park.

41

THE BODY BAG

The drawbridge lowers. Jack, obscured by the leafy forest vegetation, watches a small dark-haired girl exit the fortress. She seems to be in a hurry to leave, and quickly disappears into the woods. Just behind her stride two huge guards, one of them carrying something over his shoulder.

'What do you reckon that is? A dead body?' Jack asks Peanut, who's crouching in the bushes next to him.

'Nah, can't be; it's too small. Maybe it's something from the ruins. From what I just saw, we made a real mess of the place with that explosion.' He says this with a cheeky smirk on his face.

'Hey, look, she's back,' Jack says as the girl reappears. 'What's she up to?' They watch her hide behind a tree. *That's suspicious.*

'That is our friend, Aelianna,' Medwin whispers. 'She is the one I told you of. She must know something. Look, she waits to see what the guards are doing.'

The three sit quietly and watch, and soon they see the guards return to the fortress empty handed. The drawbridge rises behind them, and Aelianna runs into the forest, following the path the guards took to dump their load.

'Come, we must follow. She is in need of our help.' Medwin darts after her, and the boys follow.

Jack doesn't question Medwin's uncanny foresight. He's proven time and time again how accurate his visions are. Earlier tonight, he warned them that it was crucial they be by the drawbridge at sunset. He couldn't explain why, just that he trusted his sixth sense enough to drag them out into the growing darkness. Although a little dubious at first, Jack knew that he needed to put his faith in the small man. Which explains how and why they find themselves in their current situation.

They soon come upon the girl kneeling over something, sobbing uncontrollably.

Medwin approaches quietly. 'Aelianna, what has

you crying, my child?'

Aelianna gasps and looks up, startled by Medwin's sudden presence. Tears streak her face. She gasps again when she sees the two strangers with him.

'You are amongst friends. Fear not,' Medwin reassures her.

'Oh, Medwin, please, you must help me. Max is very ill. Eshmun predicts her death by the morrow!'

'Max!' Jack pushes past everyone and looks at the bundle of rags beside Aelianna. His heart skips a beat. It's Max, lying unmoving on the ground. He falls to her side. They've cut off her hair; she's lost a lot of weight, and her skin has a greyish tinge. 'What the hell have they done to her?' He gently shakes her. 'Max, come on, wake up.' She doesn't respond. He tries to sit her up, but she lays limp and heavy in his arms. 'Babe, please open your eyes.' Jack gently strokes her face. 'Geez, she's burning up. She's got a fever.'

'Fever!' Aelianna cries out. ''Tis as Ryker said. Then she will burn for her sins as Eshmun has predicted.'

'What? No, that's not true,' Jack snaps at her. 'Quick, we've got to get her to the professor. He'll know what to do.'

'Aelianna, lead the way to your home,' Medwin instructs. 'This person of whom Jack speaks is there.'

Jack carefully scoops Max up in his arms and

wastes no time in following Aelianna, who rushes through the forest before him. 'Hold on, we're almost there,' he whispers in Max's ear. He presses his lips to her temple. Alarmed at the heat of her burning skin, he picks up the pace. It feels like an eternity before they reach Aelianna's home, but finally Jack bursts through the door. 'Professor, help!'

Max's father jumps up from the patient he's been healing. His professional demeanour turns to alarm when he sees his daughter's lifeless body in Jack's arms. He stumbles backwards in shock.

Jack lays her on the bed. 'They dumped her in the forest. She's not good, doc.'

'Father, what has happened here?' Aelianna asks the other man in the room. 'How is it that you are able to stand?' She turns from him to the smiling woman sitting upright in the bed. 'Mother, what miracle is this? How is it that my family are well?'

Jack turns to the professor and sees him standing where he'd left him … frozen on the spot. 'Hey!' Jack lunges at him, grabs him by his shirt and shakes him angrily. 'What the hell are you doing? You've got to do something here!'

Max's father stares at him vacantly.

Jack searches the depths of his eyes, desperately trying to reach him. He channels all the positive energy he has to pull Max's father back from the place he's gone to. He chokes on the tears clogging his throat. 'She. Needs. You!' He watches as his words finally penetrate the professor's consciousness.

He looks down at his daughter, first with horror, and then, with sudden urgency, he bursts into action. He kneels beside the bed and begins scanning her body with the palms of his hands.

Jack staggers back, physically and mentally exhausted. It took nearly everything he had to turn the situation around.

Everyone in the room remains silent, watching on as Max's father works on her, praying that it's not too late.

Soon, a quiet moan escapes her lips. Jack hears it and drops to her side, taking her hand in his. He presses his head to hers. 'Come back, Max. I can't do this without you,' he whispers.

She twitches and her forehead wrinkles.

'Max, honey, try to open your eyes. It's daddy. I'm here.'

A single tear escapes and runs down her cheek.

Her father sweeps her up into his arms, his body trembling with uncontrollable sobs.

Totally overcome with emotion, Jack runs out of the house and takes off into the woods.

Peanut races after him. 'Hey, hold up,' he shouts.

Jack can't bear for anyone to see him like this

right now, but he slows down nonetheless.

'You okay?'

He stops, but he can't bring himself to look at Peanut, let alone answer.

'What the hell just happened?'

He finally turns to face him. 'You know something? I thought that was it ... that she was ... you know ... ' He lets out a shaky breath, unable to say it. 'I've never been so shit scared in all my life. Peanut, what if ...'

'Hey! Don't go there.'

'I don't get it. He just stood there and did nothing.'

'Yeah, I saw it. The lights were on, but he'd completely checked out.'

'What if I couldn't bring him back, Peanut? Max could've died!'

'But you did bring him back, and everything turned out in the end, right? Mate, don't beat yourself up with the *what if's*. We need to keep positive and focus on getting out of here. Half the battle's won; we've got Max back. All we need to do now is get Ryker out, and then we can quit this place for good.'

Jack looks at him ... really looks at him, as if he's seeing him for the first time. He shakes his head and grins. 'Hey, who are you, and what've you done with my best friend?'

'Oi!' Peanut says, offended. 'What's that supposed to mean? You, my friend, can thank me later!'

Jack pulls him into a man-hug. 'Thanks, mate, I mean it. I owe you one.'

'Yeah, you do … big time.' He laughs. 'And don't think I won't hold you to it.'

'So you've changed your mind about Ryker, huh? You might just stick around and save that deserter after all?' Jack grins.

'Yeah, about that, maybe I was wrong about him. He can't be too bad if he saved your girl now can he?'

Jack looks towards the little house. Aelianna and her parents exit with Medwin, talking in excited voices.

'Jack, Max is awake,' Aelianna tells him. 'I heard her ask for you.'

Jack is ready to bolt inside, but he holds back. 'Um, okay. I think I'll give her a minute with her dad.' But his nervous energy proves to be quite the challenge. He keeps distracted by focusing on the conversation around him.

'Now we must devise a plan to free Ryker,' Medwin says.

'No need, little buddy,' Peanut tells him. 'Our guys are working on that as we speak. He'll be out of there before you know it.'

'Then all that is left for us to do is to consider our

future. Do we remain, or do we leave with our new friends?' He turns to Aelianna. 'Once they free Ryker, you realise that they will need to leave at a moment's notice. Aelianna, you need to be ready if this is your wish.'

'Oh!' His words catch Aelianna off guard. Clearly, she wasn't expecting such a comment to be directed at her.

'There is no need for you to remain in this unstable world of ours, Aelianna,' her mother tells her carefully. 'As you can see, your father and I are once again well. We will remain, for now we are able to care for the children as before. We will certainly miss you, but perhaps it is time for you to follow your own dreams. These people are good people; I know it and trust them.'

Aelianna remains silent for a few moments. Everyone can see, plain as day, her internal struggle as she contemplates what to do.

Jack becomes lost in her dilemma. He can't imagine having to make such a huge decision.

Just then, Max's father calls out to him, 'Jack, Max is asking for you.'

In his haste to get to her, Jack knocks Peanut aside.

'Oi!' he shouts after him. 'Take it easy, mate! Anyone would think you're a bit keen.'

'Sorry, buddy; can't keep the lady waiting.' He darts into the little house and all but dives to Max's side.

Max is sitting upright, smiling. Seeing her like that makes his heart rate accelerate. 'Hey, you look heaps better.' He gently takes her hand and whispers, 'It's good to see you.'

'Same,' she says quietly. 'I've been worried about you.'

'You've been worried about me!' He laughs at how insane that sounds.

She squeezes his hand. 'It's good to hear you laugh. I've missed you.'

Jack's heart hammers in his chest. 'Me, too.' He leans in close and touches his forehead to hers. 'I'm just glad you're okay.' He pulls back and looks at her. Her sunken eyes and gaunt frame show how much she's suffered. 'I can't believe Ryker let this happen to you,' he says, feeling a sudden surge of anger. 'They told me you'd be safe with him, but boy, were they wrong.'

'No, Jack, don't be like that.'

'You're kidding me, right?' He jerks back. 'You're not defending him are you? Max, you nearly died because of him.'

'That's not fair.' Her eyes fill with tears. 'Ryker did what he could. If only you knew what he's been through, you'd think differently.'

Jack feels like a jerk. He knows only a little of what Ryker sacrificed for her, and it burns him hearing that there's more. *So the guy's a bloody hero!*

He doesn't know why he said what he did, and now he's gone and hurt Max. It kills him to see tears spill down her cheeks. He gathers her into his arms. 'I'm sorry, Max. You're right; I shouldn't blame him. I guess the one I'm really pissed off with is me. I feel terrible that you were left behind like that.'

'What?' She pulls away. 'Don't be an idiot! You were shot in the chest, for crying out loud! That arrow would've killed you if I hadn't removed it. I made that call. And I'll tell you this for nothing,' she pokes him in the chest, '… it was a no-brainer. You're still here because of it, and to me that's all that matters.' She wraps her arms around his neck and looks at him with tear-filled eyes. 'I couldn't bear losing you, Jack. I just couldn't!'

A movement on the other side of the room reminds them that her father is still there. 'Jack,' he says, 'I think we'd better let Max rest now; she needs to get her strength back before we leave.'

Jack jumps up, suddenly realising with embarrassment that they'd had an audience. 'Um, right, yeah. Sorry, sir.' He turns to Max and gives her a wink. 'I'll see you in the morning, then. Maybe then you can tell me what happened to your hair.'

She reaches up and pulls at the short strands, looking suddenly uncomfortable.

'Hey, I like it. It suits you.' He gives her another wink.

As Jack goes to exit the small room, Max's father calls out to him, 'And Jack,'

'Yes, sir?'

'Call me, Edward, will you? None of this *sir* stuff, okay?'

'Sure, okay. Good night … Edward.'

'Goodnight, son. And,' he pauses, '… thank you … for everything, I mean.'

Jack breathes a sigh of relief. He thought his goose was cooked following the earlier shaking incident, but clearly all that's forgiven.

He joins Peanut and Medwin, and they make their way back to the treehouse. As they walk through the forest, Jack's mind goes over his conversation with Max. He smiles, all of a sudden giddy with happiness.

'Oi, you've got that goofy smile on your face again, mate. That must've been some talk you two had,' Peanut teases.

But Jack doesn't rise to the bait. 'I wonder how Ryker's dad and Captain Logan are getting on with the plans,' he says instead. 'Too bad Ryker couldn't get himself thrown out, too, we'd be on our way home now if he had.'

'Yeah, it kinda puts a spanner in the works,' Peanut grumbles.

'Had you come a few days sooner, you would have prevented this happening,' Medwin tells them.

'Lousy timing, that's all,' Peanut says, 'But we can't change that now, can we? Hey, Medwin,' he stops suddenly, an anxious frown creasing his forehead, 'do ya reckon they've got the guards out tonight tracking us down? They'd be pretty ticked off after what we've done to their fortress again, wouldn't they?'

Medwin gives Peanut a questioning look. 'If I am to understand your meaning, Herodus would not be foolish enough to send out his men at this late hour for fear of them falling victim to the forest people.'

'Whoa, hold on a sec.' Peanut sounds panicked and his gaze darts around. 'Shouldn't we be worried then? What's stopping the savages from jumping us right now?'

Jack groans. 'Geez, Peanut, did you really just say that!' Sometimes he can't believe the things that come out of his friend's mouth. 'You bloody idiot, who the hell do you think you're with now?'

'Oh yeah,' he says awkwardly. 'Fair call. Sorry 'bout that.'

Medwin laughs. 'Be assured our people know you are here to help. We are united against the same foe. Peanut, my friend, I can honestly say that you are safe amongst the people of the forest.'

'Ya reckon!'

'Peanut!' Jack gives him another warning look.

'Look, I know *you're* okay, but no offence, what about that guy that kidnapped Max? He wasn't so friendly, was he?'

'Ah, yes. Slade is a bad seed—a lone wolf. We, too, are wary of him. But have no fear, no one has heard of him since he entered the fortress.' The little man then starts to laugh. 'I cannot understand you, Peanut. What is your concern of such things? You have the enviable gift of disappearing, have you not? This I have witnessed myself.'

'Oh, yeah. Cool, huh? I guess that's the only awesome thing about this place… you get to have superpowers. There's nothing like that where we come from.'

This pricks Medwin's attention. 'Then it is true, our special powers cease to exist once we enter your world.'

'Yeah, bummer, hey?'

They continue silently through the forest. Medwin appears deep in thought.

Back at the treehouse, they find the others sitting around a campsite fire discussing strategies.

'Ah, just the people we need to talk to,' the

vice admiral says as they approach. 'Our men have informed us that the professor's daughter has been released and is progressing well. Excellent, excellent. I am most pleased.'

Jack is surprised to hear that the news has reached them so quickly. But then again, having seen first-hand how regimented and efficient they are, he really shouldn't be. They were a force to be reckoned with before, but now they seem to be functioning at a whole different level.

'I'll say this again, Denvon,' Captain Logan interrupts the vice admiral, 'I strongly feel that we can do this without involving the kids. Let's reconsider our other options.'

'I beg to differ, Dean, there'll be no risk as long as he remains unseen. Aelianna, I feel, is no longer viable as a go-between. One of my men is questioning her as we speak. Lieutenant Goosen should be reporting back to us at any moment now. We can confidently ascertain that the enemy combatants have severed ties with the girl.'

Just then Goosen appears from the forest, breathless. He stands at attention before the vice admiral and salutes him.

'What have you learnt, Lieutenant?'

'Sir, after questioning the girl, she has confirmed our assessment of the situation. She has more than strong doubts that she will be admitted back into the fortress.'

The vice admiral turns to the group. 'Then we can't afford to waste any more time. We need to act tonight, before the enemy strike. We can't allow ourselves to become complacent. We must never underestimate the enemy.'

Jack frowns. 'I don't get it; what's the problem?'

'We need to penetrate the enemy walls and forward on information and supplies to Ryker. He needs to prepare himself for the assault,' the vice admiral explains. 'After discussions with your friends here,' he motions to Ruby and Kenny, 'I propose we send in our friend Peanut to infiltrate the enemy line and deliver this. Before you protest again Captain Logan, let the boy hear the rest of the plan.'

Captain Logan looks murderous, but bites back his objection.

'We've been trying to convince them that you'd be the best person for this, Peanut,' Kenny explains.

'Peanut knows the fortress better than anyone,' Ruby adds.

Peanut draws in a deep breath. 'Okay, hit me with it; I'm listening.'

As the vice admiral runs through the plan, Peanut listens. He keeps his head down and appears to be concentrating on every detail. At the conclusion, he doesn't hesitate to volunteer. 'No worries; I'm in. When do we start?'

'Peanut, just take a moment to think about it,' Logan suggests. 'Our success hangs on you doing this to the letter; do you understand? It'll jeopardise the whole mission, not to mention your safety, if there's even a hair's breadth of a chance that you fail. Are you absolutely certain you can do this?'

'Just get me in there, and the rest is a done-deal.'

'Peanut, are you sure?' Jack gives him another chance to back out.

But Peanut gives him his lop-sided smile. 'Piece of cake.'

42

Glue

MAX

Max is sitting up in bed with her father by her side. They talk about what's going to happen now, and every now and then, she feels him squeeze her hand as he, she imagines, tries to deal with his own tormenting demons. The grief-stricken look in his eyes says that she's close to the mark.

'You okay?'

If she had a dollar for every time he asked her this, she'd be laughing all the way to the bank. But she doesn't say a word. She just smiles sympathetically and squeezes his hand back. How she has missed that simple pleasure of just holding his hand. Suddenly the problems of the world don't seem so daunting.

Aelianna enters the home after her brief talk to one of the taskforce members. 'The lovely man was just asking after my well-being,' she tells them. 'And also if there was the possibility that I could assist them further with Ryker if need be.' Her face glows as she says his name.

'I hope you said no, Aelianna,' Max says. 'Please don't feel that you need to do anything more than you already have. They'll manage to get him out on their own.'

'But I am happy to,' she says, a little deflated.

Max's father stands and goes to her. 'You've placed yourself at great risk to help save my daughter,' he tells her sincerely, 'and for that I'll be eternally grateful. But now, you must leave it to the squad to get him out.'

'I must agree to that,' Aelianna's father says. 'Your mother and I are both very proud of you, daughter, for you have shown great strength and spirit. But now you must become even more courageous and make your decision … to go with our new friends, or to stay.'

Aelianna's eyes go wide with indecision.

A knock sounds on the door. They share anxious looks, but Medwin's familiar voice outside averts a panic.

Max's heart skips a beat when Jack enters with

him.

'Forgive the late intrusion,' Medwin begins, 'but we need to act hastily. There are developments in place for Ryker's release.'

Jack sits by Max's side and takes her hand. 'We've come to take you and your dad back with us so we can be ready to go as soon as he's out. Do you think you're okay to come back with us?'

She tells him she is.

He then runs through the plan, explaining that if all goes well with Peanut tonight, they should be ready to leave first thing in the morning.

While she sits there watching him talk, she realises that the butterflies in her stomach have nothing to do with the news that they're finally close to going home. Just having Jack so near her is doing that. She looks down at their clasped hands, then back at his smiling face. His eyes are taking her in with a look that she's never seen before. Her heart skips a beat.

She then realises that he's once again taking in her clipped hair. She withdraws her hand.

'Hey,' he whispers, 'what's up?'

She self-consciously tugs at the short strands, then looks anxiously at Aelianna, praying that she doesn't say anything.

Jack takes her hand in his to stop her from pulling at her hair and tells her again that he likes it. 'Hey, what can I say … you look cute with shorter hair. And if you decide that you don't like it, it's not as if it won't grow back, right?'

Max's heart sinks. She wonders how vain he must think she is … worrying about her stupid hair. But then she feels the need to explain, and so she tells him.

Aelianna joins them on the bed and helps Max fill in some of the details. Both Jack and her father sit with horror growing in their eyes as they hear about her ordeal. Max's father starts to tear up, knowing now what his daughter had suffered, but Jack, her Jack, cups her face in his hands and tells her that she's the most beautiful girl that he's ever seen.

43

A Chip Off The Old Block

Ryker

A hard smack to the head wakes Ryker. Momentarily disorientated, he sits up and looks around the empty room. He receives another hit, and something bounces on the bed.

'What the hell!' He rubs his head and looks at the object. A small rock lies on the bed next to him. He picks it up and studies it like he's never seen one before.

'Pssst! Pssst!'

Suddenly Ryker is wide awake. 'Peanut? Hey, you're back.' He goes to the window. 'What's happening? What's the plan?'

'Shh! Will ya shut up! D'ya want the whole world to know I'm here? Friggin unbelievable! *Survival training,* my arse,' Peanut grumbles under his breath.

Ryker chuckles. He's so inexplicably happy that he forgot himself for a moment.

'Now listen carefully,' Peanut says, suddenly serious, 'because I don't have time to explain this twice, and also because I wanna get everything right so your dad doesn't kick my butt.'

Ryker's heart feels like it jumps into his throat. 'My father's here?'

'Did I forget to mention that before?' Peanut chuckles. 'Yeah, well, he kind'a thinks that he's running the whole shebang. You never mentioned that he was such a big-wig. He's got the whole squad jumping to his command. He even has Logan fighting to get a word in edgeways—and he's the one that's supposed to be in charge.'

Ryker can't believe it. His dad is here.

'Hey, you okay, mate? Great news, huh? I thought you'd get a buzz from hearing that. Man, he misses you. I'm surprised he hasn't already come charging in here, guns blazing, to get you out. I guess we gotta do this right, like Logan says.'

Ryker chokes up a little.

'It's been too long, mate. C'mon, we need to get

you home.'

Tears distort Ryker's vision. But enough of that. He needs to keep it together. There's nothing in this world that's going to stop him from seeing his father again. He snaps into tactical mode. 'Peanut, tell me exactly what my father's told you. What do I have to do?'

Peanut quickly, but methodically, runs through the plan. Ryker remains still and focused, his breathing deepening as he takes in every detail. He doesn't allow his thoughts to deviate from Peanut's instructions.

Once he's finished, a backpack appears, literally out of nowhere, and squeezes into the small window frame. Ryker grabs it and pulls it through. He figures it must have been hidden beneath Peanut's invisible clothes.

'I've been told you'll have no trouble managing the stuff in there,' Peanut tells him. 'Man, you've had an interesting childhood; I'll give you that much.'

Ryker rummages through the backpack. 'Yeah, I'm good with this,' he confirms. 'Thanks, Peanut; I owe you one. You okay getting back?'

'No worries. You know, if I could smuggle you under my shirt, we could both get the hell out of here. I'd wish you good luck, but after seeing what's in that bag of goodies, I don't think you'll need it.

Mate, we'll be home before you know it.'

'Never underestimate the enemy, Peanut. We can't afford to become complacent.'

Peanut chuckles quietly to himself. 'You're the spit out of your dad's mouth, you know that?'

'Spit out of what?' Peanut's odd way of saying things once again stumps Ryker.

'Maybe you've heard the saying *the apple doesn't fall far from the tree* or *cut from the same cloth*? What I'm trying to say … look, that crap doesn't really matter, we've got stuff to do.'

'Yeah, go. And Peanut, I mean it, we can't afford to let our defences down. Vigilant at all times.'

'No worries, mate. You can count on me.'

And suddenly Peanut is gone.

Ryker scans the forest, looking for any signs of his movement. He strains his ears trying to hear any sounds of his retreat … but nothing. Ryker smiles and shakes his head. 'Go figure … who would've thought he had it in him?'

But there's work to be done, so he needs to knuckle down and get on with it. His focus shifts, and he spends the next few hours going over his father's instructions. He recreates various scenarios in his head and agonises over strategies to counter attack every possible situation.

Preparation is crucial for success ... expect the unexpected ... failure is not an option. He keeps repeating the mantra in his head until, well into the night, he finally falls asleep.

44

Let's Do This

Ryker

Ryker wakes after a short recharging nap, anxious to put the plan into action. It must be close to dawn. Although still dark outside, he can hear the forest animals preparing for the new day. The time is right. He knows his father is waiting for him to make the first move.

He tries the chamber door and, as he suspected, it's bolted shut. After last night's dramas, he's not surprised. He may have won over Archimedes and the others, but Herodus is another story. His keen eye doesn't miss a thing.

No worries; I've got just the thing.

He grabs the backpack and rummages through

it to find a block of putty, some electric wire and a small detonator. He attaches the wires to the detonator and, with careful precision, manipulates the putty to fashion a small explosive that he then moulds securely around the base of the central bar of the chamber window.

He's ready.

He starts the detonator timer, pulls a gas mask out of the bag and secures it on top of his head, then swings the backpack over his shoulders. With the calm of a professional explosives expert, Ryker moves to the back corner of the chamber, grabbing the bedding and the small table to shield himself from the anticipated blast.

Just as he crouches behind the protective barrier, the detonator triggers, and a loud explosion blasts a hole in the wall big enough to allow Ryker to make his escape. He throws off the table and bedding, debris from the explosion scattering everywhere. Within seconds he's out, completely unharmed.

With a compass clasped tightly in his hand, he moves swiftly through the garden, his destination the fortress wall. His father waits on the other side of that wall. But he can't let that distract him. Anything could still happen.

Expect the unexpected!

45

The Gods Have Spoken

Herodus

The echoes of an explosion ricochet down the passageway, waking Herodus from his sleep. With his heart pounding in his chest, he shouts out to his guards to prepare themselves for an attack, then he runs to the chambers of the Invincibles to pull together his strongest offensive. On opening Ryker's door, he is met with a confusing sight. The room is in ruins, and there's no sign of the boy. It takes Herodus two seconds to realise what has happened here. How Ryker did it is beyond his comprehension, but why he did it is not.

'Traitor! Search for him. This is not an attack; it is an escape.'

He and his men are about to charge through the demolished wall when they hear a commanding voice booming from afar. They stop, frozen in place, to listen.

'This is Captain Dean Logan from the Australian Defence Force requesting that you release the prisoner Ryker Engelbrecht into my custody immediately.'

Herodus looks around him, then at his men, dumb-founded. *What are these strange words, and from where do they come?* Shaking himself into action, he shouts his commands. 'Athos, take the others and hunt down Ryker. And when you catch him, kill him. The rest of you, follow me.'

Herodus takes off to the arena, prepared to face whatever onslaught awaits them there. They enter with swords raised and war cries on their lips, then stop abruptly ... there isn't a soul there. Herodus looks around, bewildered. 'What is this trickery?'

And then the voice booms again. 'I repeat, this is Captain Dean Logan from the Australian Defence Force requesting that you release the prisoner Ryker Engelbrecht to my custody immediately. Let down your drawbridge.'

Herodus frowns in confusion. 'What kind of

black magic is this?' He calls up to the guard in the tower overlooking the forest. 'What do you see?'

'Sir, I see nothing. I know not from where the voice is coming.'

Captain Logan's voice carries, once again, across to them. 'This is your final warning.'

Herodus has no idea what he's meant to do.

Just then, Eshmun runs into the arena, half dressed and in a panic. 'You fool; 'tis the Gods that are hailing us. Why do you just stand there? Lower the drawbridge!'

The Gods!

In a panic, Herodus calls up to the heavens in fear, 'The man you seek has escaped; he is no longer a captive.'

But his pleas fall on deaf ears. A loud explosion shakes the ground beneath them and the drawbridge collapses. Debris and dust obscure the view for several moments, then three uniformed men wearing strange masks and carrying weapons spouting flames emerge from the dust. The small group approach the fortress's stunned defence.

Herodus takes a few steps back. He has never seen anything like this.

Eshmun throws himself to the ground.

The five Ancients arrive in time to witness Eshmun's submission. 'What is the meaning of this?'

Pius cries out. 'Herodus, why do you stand there doing nothing? Attack!'

'Stop, or we will be forced to defend ourselves,' Captain Logan's voice booms once more.

Herodus commands an attack. His guards, armed with swords, knives and spears, charge the invaders. But the attackers throw objects that spew out some kind of toxic gas. The guards double-over, coughing, heaving and retching. They cry out in pain and rub at their eyes and throats.

'Attack! Attack!' the Ancients' yell.

On their command, two of the guards push through their suffering.

'Stop or we will be forced to defend ourselves,' the voice warns again.

More guards recover and re-enter the attack, but the attackers throw even more of their evil packages, halting the guards' defence once again. Many retreat out of fear.

Herodus turns to seek instruction from the Ancients, but finds himself alone. Before he has time to rethink his plan of attack, flames roar towards them, forcing them to retreat further. Clearly, they have no hope. Gods or not, these people seeking Ryker have powers beyond anything he has ever seen.

'Cease attack! I will call off my guards.'

The flames are immediately extinguished.

46

SHOWTIME

RYKER

Vigilant at all times ... expect the unexpected ... Ryker repeats his mantra to himself as he carefully weaves his way through the garden. Hopefully the decoy to buy him enough time to get away has been a success, but regardless, he needs to get away as fast as possible. Even with the squad creating a smokescreen to distract Herodus, he doesn't have that much time.

His escape movement is one they'll least likely expect him to make. They'll anticipate that he'll head for the newly blasted hole in the fortress wall, but knowing that the exit will be heavily guarded, Ryker deliberately avoids taking that option and heads in the opposite direction. If he can lose his tail even for a few minutes, it might be the head start he needs.

As he races to his destination, he hopes Herodus has enlisted the Invincibles as back-up and gone straight to the arena with them. But when he spots something flying in the distance, he realises that he didn't. It's Vyvian. He dives for cover and monitors her aerial movements.

From what he can see, she hasn't spotted him yet. So he's got a little time to calculate his next move. He takes a moment … he's got to get this right. Timing is crucial, and there's no room for error. Once he's set on what he needs to do, he goes over his plan once more. Satisfied that it's solid, he reaches into his backpack, pulls out a smoke-screen grenade and peers from his cover to locate her position. When he's confident that it's safe to take action, he pelts the grenade in the direction of the arena. The canister immediately deploys with a volume of smoke that rises above the forest.

His plan to send her backtracking works. Vyvian notices the disturbance and darts over to investigate.

Ryker figures the other three will be monitoring her and so will follow. He anticipates that, once together, Shant will act next. It's a calculated risk, but one he's confident will work. And moments later, he isn't disappointed. A sudden gale, conjured out of thin air, blows away the smoke cloud.

Reassured that he's grouped them together, Ryker pelts another two grenades in the same direction—this time tear-gas grenades. He knows he's hit his mark when he hears a chorus of coughing and screaming as they cry out in pain.

It's time for Ryker to make his move. He dives out of his hiding place and takes off like a bat out of hell. He only hopes that he's given himself a sufficient head start. His heart races as he tears through the outer garden—a garden he knows only too well, having memorised every square inch of it over the years, and one that, all of a sudden, seems endless.

And then he finally sees it … the fortress wall. He lets off a flare to notify the squad of his arrival and then begins the countdown. He needs to act swiftly after this—the flare will immediately attract the enemy. But it's a risk he's willing to take. He looks around for his best option for cover, then crouches low, shields his head with his backpack and prepares for the explosion.

Five, four, three, two, one … BOOM!

The blast leaves the air thick with smoke and debris, but Ryker wastes no time. He pulls down his mask and runs towards the hole in the wall. He can see three figures standing on the other side: two ready with flamethrowers, and one solitary figure standing between them. Even with obscured visibility, Ryker recognises that figure and runs straight into his open arms.

Knowing that time is of the essence, they both pull out of the embrace.

'I've got four on my tail,' Ryker informs them.

'The Invincibles,' his father says. 'Yes, we've been informed.' He turns to his men, 'Goosen, De Beer, get ready.'

Ryker catches Vyvian in his sights and points her out to the flamethrowers. Before she has time to fire an arrow at them, both soldiers fire a heated blast at her. A terrifying scream of pain tells them that they've hit their mark.

'Run!' Ryker yells. 'The others won't be far.'

They take off into the woods.

A sudden, thunderous rumble shakes the earth, driving a mass-evacuation of hundreds of birds into the sky. Without warning, the wind picks up to gale proportions, threatening to uproot the trees in their path.

'Keep going, son; we'll hold them off,' his father yells against the howling winds.

'Not without you!'

The enemy gains ground. Ryker can see Shant, his arms raised, controlling the gale.

Archimedes is close behind. Ryker senses him before he sees him. His thoughts are suddenly no longer his own. And just as quickly as he realises this, Ryker falls to the ground, writhing in excruciating pain. He blocks him out, and over the howling wind, he calls out the warning to the others. 'Archimedes is getting into our heads. Sing! Singing jams his reception.'

But they soon realise that it's not Archimedes they need to worry about. Shant's tactics have slowed their escape to a snail's pace. They're virtually crawling on all fours, trying to get away. The flamethrowers are useless in these conditions. The situation has taken a turn for the worse.

Goosen attempts to throw a grenade at them, but it backfires and detonates dangerously too close to them. De Beer also prepares to retaliate, his firearm at the ready.

'Hold back your fire!' their commander orders.

Ryker is struggling to find a way out of this disaster. Grenades and ammunition aren't going to make any impact in this situation. They need a miracle to have a chance to fight back.

And suddenly that miracle arrives in the form of a spirited red head. Out of the blue, Ruby appears in all her glory and uses the force of her magnificent shield to repel the gale force winds.

'Ruby!' Ryker cheers. He watches the look on Shant's smug face slowly turn to desperation as he starts to lose control.

'Whoohoo! You go girl!'

Ruby's confidence soars. Within moments she has Shant struggling to fight back.

With Shant showing signs of defeat, and Archimedes's efforts blocked at every turn, Ryker turns his attention to the final Invincible, Athos, who has, until now, taken a back seat in the attack. Ryker knows he needs to act now before Athos picks up momentum. But before he has a chance to do anything, a large branch flies towards Athos and smacks him on the back of his head, knocking the old man flat on his face, out cold.

Peanut materialises before his prone form. 'Hey, you've left your run a little too late, mate!' he cries out triumphantly. 'Not so invincible now, are ya?'

Ryker charges towards Peanut and crash tackles him to the ground, laughing. 'What a legend!'

Captain Logan and his men arrive at that moment, and Gallo is quick to use his newfound power to assist Ruby. Together, with her brilliant shield and the force of his telekinetic ability, they quickly overpower Shant, and have him stumbling backwards, defeated.

A few detonating stun grenades aimed in the right direction by Logan puts a complete halt to the attack. They hear cries of agony as the victims struggle to deal with the blinding and deafening effects of the grenades.

Logan wastes no time. 'To the portal, now!'

Ryker snaps out of his premature euphoria and starts to run. Their escape is within reach. One more hurdle and they'll be safe. They're bound to come across the portal guards at any moment. *Vigilant at all times!* He scans his surrounds as he tears through the forest. He can't afford to be complacent this close to the finish line. They're nearing the gateway, almost there. Ryker has his defences up and is prepared to fight for their passage. But something's not right … things are too quiet. He slows his approach, holding his hands up, cautioning the others.

But his alarm vanishes when he sees Medwin appear from the forest, smiling mischievously. 'Calm yourself, there is no threat.'

'Nor will there be,' Jack laughs as he appears from hiding with the rest of the gang. 'The people of the forest have taken care of that.'

Ryker now notices several guards strewn across the ground, bound and unconscious. The forest suddenly comes alive with activity, revealing the many village people hidden there. Ten, twenty, thirty forest people emerge.

Ryker's relief is huge. He grabs Medwin in an appreciative embrace, and the smaller man struggles to loosen his hold. 'I too am pleased to see you again, my friend, but now you must release me before you crush the life from me.'

Ryker laughs. He then considers all the people on the fringes of the forest that have just helped save their lives. 'So are all these people coming back with us?'

His excitement skyrockets when he notices Aelianna and her family amongst the crowd. His heart almost explodes at the sight of her. But he's quick to rein in his emotions to focus on what needs to be done. 'Okay, so that's a few more than what we were expecting, but it is what it is. Let's get out of here.' He makes to leave but notices that the villagers aren't following. 'Guys, we need to go. Now.'

'Son,' Ryker's father approaches him, 'we can't wait any longer.'

'Medwin, what's going on? You're coming, right?'

'Ryker, this is our home,' Medwin says, 'and this is all we know. You come from a world I fear will be too challenging for the likes of us. I must admit, at first I found the idea of a new beginning appealing, but my destiny is to remain here. This I know is the right thing to do, and I have made peace with my decision. I fear that I will be sacrificing too much if I were to follow you. Please understand, my gift has been my steadfast companion for all of my life.'

Ryker turns to Aelianna. 'But will none of you come?'

Aelianna looks away. A single tear spills down her cheek. He watches her struggle to tell him. But he already knows her answer. Deep down, he understands. Her decision would have been a difficult one to make, and he needs to respect that.

She steps forward, takes his hands in hers and raises them to her lips. Then without a word, she steps away and disappears into the forest.

He looks down at the small red flower she has left in his palm.

'People, we need to leave immediately!' Logan warns. The urgency of the command snaps Ryker back to the potential threat they're still exposed to.

Peanut doesn't need to be told twice, he takes Ruby's hand and squeezes it. 'Ready?'

'You bet! Let's get out of here.'

And as quick as that, they're gone, vanished through the gateway.

Jack turns to face Max. 'You're going before me this time.'

She's about to argue, but Jack cuts her off, 'No buts. Edward can you please take this pain in the neck and go!'

'Come on sweetheart, you heard the man.'

Ryker watches as Max finally passes through the

wispy veil. He lets out a sigh of relief. 'Man, that was a long time coming.'

Jack smiles knowingly at him. He pulls him into a man-hug before turning to exit. Kenny follows closely behind. Captain Logan motions for the vice admiral to go next.

Ryker's father salutes the captain, honouring him with the utmost respect. 'You can be proud of your efforts Captain Logan,' he says formally, but the mask of ceremony quickly disappears with an unexpected smile that transforms his whole demeanour, 'but I won't be passing through until I've seen the squad safe. After you, son.'

Clearly not expecting this, Logan reluctantly beckons for his men to pass through before following at the rear.

Before exiting the ancient realm, Ryker stops for a moment to have a final look at this diaphanous phenomenon before him.

The vice admiral stands by his side and places a fatherly hand on his shoulder. 'Never in all my years have I seen anything so beautiful, yet so formidable. Come on, son, let's go home; your mother is waiting.'

With his eyes wide open, Ryker slowly crosses through the gossamer veil, praying that his passage through it will be the final one that this realm will ever witness again.

A Note From The Author

Did you enjoy my book?

If so, I would be very grateful if you could write a review and publish it at your point of purchase. Your review, even a brief one, will help other readers to decide whether or not they'll enjoy my work.

Realm Travellers – A Parallel Dimension is the sequel to *Realm Travellers – The Ancient Gateway*, and is the second book in this series of low-fantasy novels. If you'd like to be notified of the publication of new books in this series, please sign up to my email list. You'll find the sign-up button on the M.J. Raco, Author page on Facebook.

www.ingramcontent.com/pod-product-compliance
Lightning Source LLC
Chambersburg PA
CBHW060903190726
48286CB00002B/357